Letters from the Flesh

–Marcos Donnelly–

Robert J.
SAWYER
BOOKS

Robert J. Sawyer Books are published by
Red Deer Press
813 MacKimmie Library Tower
2500 University Drive N.W.
Calgary Alberta Canada T2N 1N4
www.reddeerpress.com

Credits
Edited for the Press by Robert J. Sawyer
Cover and text design by Erin Woodward
Cover illustration by Sam Weber
Cover photo courtesy of Hubble Space Telescope Science Institute
Printed and bound in Canada by Friesens for Red Deer Press

National Library of Canada Cataloguing in Publication
Donnelly, Marcos
Letters from the flesh / Marcos Donnelly ; editor, Robert J. Sawyer.
ISBN 0-88995-302-3
I. Sawyer, Robert J. II. Title.
PS3554.O5495L48 2004   813'.54   C2004-900623-1

For Vikki, who believes
some things happen for a reason.
Not all things . . . just some.

—Acknowledgements—

Special thanks to the first-draft readers whose feedback helped shape this work: Dr. Virginia Mitchell, Dr. Barbara Grosh, David Neimeyer, and R. P. Siegel.

—Introduction—

A new idea took hold back in the twentieth century, popularized by such figures as paleontologist Stephen Jay Gould and astronomer Carl Sagan: science and religion are antithetical; one has nothing to do with the other.

Ironically, science fiction—a literature that developed in that same now-gone century—has rarely heeded the Gould-Sagan injunction. Even Sagan's own science-fiction novel, *Contact,* ends with incontrovertible proof of God's existence being found via scientific means (a scene criminally not included in the film based on the novel).

Granted, many science-fictional treatments of religion are simplistic. For all their popularity, neither Arthur C. Clarke's story "The Star" nor his "The Nine Billion Names of God" bears serious scrutiny. But other SF writers (or "fanciful supposers," to use the author of the present volume's poetic term for them) have had much that is both scientifically and theologically interesting to say: Karel Capek in *The Absolute at Large;* Olaf Stapeldon in *Star Maker;* James Blish, in the Hugo Award-winning *A Case of Conscience;* Walter M. Miller, Jr., in *A Canticle for Liebowitz;* Michael Moorcock in *Behold The Man;* Mary Doria Russell in *The Sparrow;* James Morrow in *Only Begotten Daughter;* even (some critics have been kind enough to note) myself in *Calculating God.*

And now we can add Marcos Donnelly to this list. In *Letters from the Flesh*—a witty homage to C. S. Lewis's *The Screwtape Letters*—Donnelly tackles the hot-button issue of evolution versus creationism, while giving us first-hand testimony from an alien observer who was on hand at the time of Christ. Satiric and insightful, *Letters from the Flesh* is informed by encyclopedic knowledge of both science and theology. It's in the very best tradition of idea-driven science fiction, and is a perfect exemplar of the sort of literate, philosophically rich, mind-expanding books Red Deer Press and I hope to bring to you under this new imprint.

–Robert J. Sawyer

January 2004

—Preface—

I have no intention of explaining how the dual sets of letters found in this volume happened to appear, unsolicited, in my email.

But this I will say, by way of preface: there are two types of errors about Creationism into which lovers of science can fall. The first is to completely ignore anything a Creationist has to say about the nature of the universe. The other is to allow oneself to become so obsessed with combating Creationism that one becomes lost in endless Creationist rhetoric and quasi-scientific objections to the still-developing theory of evolution. Creationists are equally comfortable dealing with both these approaches, hailing the first as proof of atheism and the second as evidence of agnosticism. Readers could easily find the sorts of arguments underlying the epistles published here at any Creationist Web site; but ill-disposed or excitable science lovers who might make bad use of those sites shall not learn the URLs from me.

Readers are advised to remember that scientists can get very defensive about their territories. Not everything that Doctor Lillian says on the following pages should be taken at face value. Nor should the perceptions of the Asarkos alien authoring the second set of epistles be trusted without reservation. I've made no attempt to rebut or confirm any of the scientific explanations either letter writer provides; but I think it highly unlikely that the universe really is, exactly, just how each describes it. There are principles of Faith in science, just as there are in Creationism.

In conclusion, I ought to comment that the chronology of the letters is a little distracting, but that I've made no efforts to re-sort them. Lillian's emails appear to be from a time after established, widespread use of the Internet, probably dating from quite late in the 20th century; the Asarkos epistles most likely date from after Herod Agrippa was appointed by Rome to his throne as king of the Tetrarchy, *Anno Domini* 40 or 41. But a human-system date like that, except insofar as it happened to affect him in his newly acquired flesh persona, would obviously mean little to the formerly bodiless Asarkos.

"My dear Wormwood,

"Humans are amphibians, half spirit and half animal. As spirits they belong to the eternal world, but as animals they inhabit time."

"My dear Wormwood,

"I note with grave displeasure that your patient has become a Christian."

–C.S. Lewis
The Screwtape Letters

—1—

To you who are my kind,

Romans, Greeks, Hebrews, Judeans, Samaritans . . . words, words all around me, but I have no way to tell you what has happened. I have no news of The Ten, or of what has become of them. I have a great deal of other information, but most of it is still incomprehensible to me. Calling things by names seems to be very important here. I am at a place that is called Damascus, but it is also called Syria. I apparently work for a "king," the highest member of a grouping here, that is named Herod Agrippa. But there is another king that is sometimes named Caesar, sometimes named Gaius Caligula, and sometimes named both. Caligula is king over the other king, and I am befuddled. They may not define the term "highest" as we do. They are built of matter, after all, and are like nothing we have ever encountered.

Our science was wrong. Our fanciful supposers were right, our brethren to whom we insisted that "that sort of thing" just couldn't be true, couldn't be real. These beings are alive, sentient, and intelligent, even though they are made of matter. We have been so arrogant. We never suspected compositions built from particles could be alive and aware. But I have now confirmed a third sentient race in our universe.

I am not accustomed to feeling befuddled. Nor am I accustomed to losing track of information. They tell me words, and in confusion I forget many of them. I think the information is stored in their highest matter cluster, positioned in their heads. That is where I sense myself being, now that I am encased in one of these creatures of matter. Maybe only limited data can be held in a head. I don't know. I forget much, and must have my new friend record for me as I speak, as I am having him do right now with this epistle. There is no way for you to access this, of course; there is no way for me to access it either, but my friend will keep telling me what I have said because of my need to remember. I cannot yet explain how the recording of thoughts and events is done here, but these ones, these matter-made sentients, call it *writing*. My new friend is named Judah. He protests that I am not using proper form to have him record who is writing my information, but I want to remember to tell you all things.

Judah names me Saul of Tarsus, but already wants to call me by a different name. He says the old term Saul (old to him, new to me) makes me the namesake of an ancient, arrogant king, but that the name he now chooses for me, "Paul," means "humble." When I ask him why he wishes to call me humble, he says it is because I have met the Risen Christ on the road to Damascus. When I ask him what a Risen Christ is, he says that it is the King of all Kings, Lord of all Lords.

This is a race quite enamored of their kings.

I am to *sign* this epistle with my name. Judah will guide me, and I will feel what he calls his *hands* on what now are presumably my *hands*. But I realize I have no name that you recognize by our customs. (We must consider adopting the custom of names.) Before today, we knew only of two sentient races: ourselves, and Our Enemies, all the distinction we needed. Now we see mind in matter . . . *sarx*, Judah calls it, "flesh" in the language of the wise Greek groupings here. You are my Not-Flesh race, my *a-sarx*, so I shall call us the Asarkos. This race of sentient matter I call the fleshed ones, the Sarkate. And myself, I shall be called according to the wishes of my first friend here.

I am tired now, but there shall be much more later.

Yours from among the Sarkate,

Paul of Tarsus

SENT BY: Lillian.Uberland@rsi.edu
RECEIVED BY: MNA@sellenville.edu

Kiss-Kiss, Cousin!

Well, knock me over. Little Mikey finally has himself an email address! You know what this means, of course. I get to keep dishing out all the brilliant advice you've come to rely on over the years. Plus, you're spared the bother of driving all the way into the city to visit me face-to-face. Isn't it beautiful? You get the benefits of my four extra years of life experience, plus more spending money from the gas you'll save, all through one little online connection.

Right to it then; this girl *never* ignores her advice-giving responsibilities. The troubles you're having with the handful of Fundamentalist students in your Biology class shouldn't have come as a surprise to you. What did you expect, landing your first teaching job in an outskirts suburb like Sellenville? I know it's not a rural Bible-belt public school (those people wouldn't have hired an evil evolutionist sympathizer like you in the first place), but it's close enough to the sticks that it should have made you cautious.

You say you've given the Fundamentalist kids some additional reading material on the basics of evolution. But aren't you being just a little bit naive? It sounds like you think that facts are enough to snatch them from the clutches of Creationist beliefs. That might have been true if you were dealing with a rational group of people, but you've got to remember that these kids are immersed in the jargon of their Fundamentalist parents. They've been raised to think of things as Definitely True or Definitely False, and they've been handed all the "correct" conclusions beforehand. In their world, conclusions come first, facts are an afterthought.

Sad as it sounds, you're years too late to convince a bunch of Creationist tenth graders that science could ever, ever offer any important truth that isn't already found in their Holy Scriptures. I'm sure you've run into one of my favorite snippets of Creationist jargon: "Evolution is just a theory!" Since they've always heard their Scriptures called "truth," and they've always heard us call evolution a "theory," we lose the semantics game. To them, it's obvious. We're guessing; they're right.

Gravity's just a theory, too. Shall we throw them all out a window and show them how it works?

All right, that was harsh, I guess. But never forget: dedicated Christians have a long, honored history of killing scientists like us for our contradictions of the Faith. Scientists, on the other hand, hardly ever burn people for violations of reason.

(See how nice I'm being to you, Mikey? I include you among scientists, even though you abandoned the Ph.D. track to become a high school science teacher. No, don't thank me, I'm naturally generous . . . although that's *Doctor* Generous to you, you slacker.)

Seriously, Mikey, don't get mixed up in arguing with a tiny group of anti-science religionist kids. You're in school to teach the other ones. Leave the Creationists alone, and one day, when the world has become a touch more rational, they'll have quietly disappeared into their tiny, faith-filled universes, awash in the peculiar kind of empty clarity which religion affords. If you try to sway them, you only risk attracting the attention of their parents. And believe me, you don't want to go there.

Tell me about more important things, like whether you're dating anyone interesting yet!

Your affectionate cousin,

Doctor (ahem!) Lillian

—3—

Greetings to my kind, the No-Flesh Asarkos,

Apparently I am blind, or so says my Sarkate friend and companion Judah. He says that if I were not, I would be able to see these writings he is creating on my behalf. His explanations are crude, but I believe I can deduce his deeper meanings.

In the Sarkate, the uppermost matter cluster called the head accommodates two elements called eyes. These eyes are supposed to collect waves from my environs and translate them into dimensional images which the matter in my head interprets, allowing the mobile portions of my body to navigate the planet floor. Since none of this "seeing" is presently occurring for me, I can only theorize that the phenomenon is analogous to our own electrolocation capabilities. But the functionality for the matter beings seems reversed: whereas we radiate our own excretory waves and interpret their echoes as we move through the cosmos, the Sarkate actually absorb energies into themselves. Those energies come primarily from the star that hosts their planet, and their eyes use the radiation to "see." Their skin takes in the energy to "warm." Who knows how else they use the energies and spectra that make up our reality of the wave-filled cosmos?

(I have had to explain at length some of the words I use, and my friend Judah does his best to transcribe them accurately. Please forgive terminology you find too vague or anomalous.)

These ponderings on the creatures of matter lead me to more mysteries: since I have been absorbed by the eyes and skin of this creature of matter, why am I still in existence? Why wasn't I nullified, as when one of Our Enemies effectively assaults us, or (to use a Sarkate comparison) simply consumed like so much ingested food? And more: what became of the sentience of Saul, now Paul, of Tarsus? For I do not sense him dwelling within the flesh now encasing me.

Mystery upon mystery upon mystery in this world where Caesar and Christ are both king. I should be more thorough here, in case one day I am able to read you these epistles. I shall have Judah record the things I know, rather than have him labor over my declarations of ignorance.

Here are facts.

As commanded by my assignment, I was investigating this area of the cosmos for some sign of The Ten Who Are Missing. Also in keeping with my assignment, I was collecting data for later evaluation by those who are skilled in the practice of our sciences. I confess I strayed somewhat . . . not to neglect my duties, but to explore side interests, gathering data above and beyond my assignment. In honesty, I had heard of this place, this planet on which I now reside, and I had been intrigued by reports of the mutability and mobility of its matter structures. To examine them more closely, I accelerated my own wavelength, echoing my radiant emanations off decreasingly smaller particles of matter.

I must here defend myself, I know. I am a sensible member of our kind, and I am fully aware that we of the Asarkos race never tempt ourselves to explore the higher, tighter wave frequencies. Those frequencies are where Our Enemies operate. I know the risks. I know the consequences. And if any of my Asarkos brethren are pleased to hear so, I received my due: the moment I achieved a modulation of eight Roman cubits, Our Enemies appeared around me, in greater numbers than I ever imagined possible. I believe I surprised them, for they did not act immediately to eradicate me. And I fled . . . but I feared they would follow me toward the lower frequencies, stopping me before I reached the safe ranges that give us refuge. I tricked them by making my escape in the unexpected direction. I went to higher frequencies still.

I realize this is unthinkable. I was not, however, thinking, simply fleeing.

It worked; they lost track of me immediately, and I, for my part, found this world. At 1800 nanocubits of wavelength, I noticed the change: the moving matter came apparent to me as discrete units. At 1400 nanocubits, I detected the Sarkate, and noted their difference from other matter structures. It was at 700 nanocubits that the matter-based Sarkate detected me. Saul of Tarsus "saw" me first, and it was to him I was drawn by a force rivaling that of a collapsed, self-swallowed matter star.

For a time after that, I recall nothing. My friend Judah describes it this way, in his words:

"Saul of Tarsus came along the road to Damascus, breathing threats of violence and murder against those who believe in the Risen Christ. He carried with him letters of introduction from the Jewish Council, that the leaders of the community in Damascus might know that he came with the blessing of the High Priest. And we, the believers of Christ in Damascus, were afraid, for this very Saul had officiated over the stoning death of our brother Stephen, and had arrested and persecuted many believers in Jerusalem.

"As Saul and three companions approached Damascus, great flashes of light from the sky surrounded him, and he fell to the ground. His companions heard Saul praying and lamenting in Hebrew, and then in Greek, then Latin, then in many more languages the companions did not understand. When the light left him, Saul was blind and did not speak. So the companions led him by the hand into Damascus and brought him to my home, for I am a physician of this city.

"I was filled with terror, for unbeknownst to Saul's companions I am a believer in the Risen Christ our Lord, and here in my home was the man whose coming terrified the brethren.

"But for two days he did not speak, nor did he eat, as if he were weighing in his heart the events that had befallen him. Great scales had grown over his eyes, and his companions grew weary of his silence. They left him in my care, and went to the community leaders of the Jews to ask what must become of their mission now that Saul of Tarsus had been blinded and dumbstruck by an angel of the Lord.

"The day after they left, Saul finally spoke. My beloved wife Esther, for whom I have feared since the day we had news that this Saul of Tarsus had seen to the death of our brother Stephen, was again trying to make Saul eat. She was ordering him to accept food, but behind her commanding tone there was compassion. She, like me, had been moved to pity for this passive, helpless, blinded persecutor of our Faith.

"She touched his face to try to open his mouth, and it was then we were startled by his voice. 'What has happened to me?' he asked Esther.

"Esther drew back frightened, as if she had woken a sleeping monster. I came to her side, and my faith filled me with courage. 'Saul of Tarsus,' I said, 'why do you persecute us?'

"'Who are you, sir?' he asked.

"'I am Judah, one of those whom you persecute.'

"Esther was overcome with fear, for I had told the enemy my name, and had informed him that we were the very sheep he strove to slaughter. But she was calmed when Saul humbly asked, 'What has become of me? What must I do?'

"I wanted to tell him that he must accept the word of the Risen Christ, for I understood that it was our Lord who had appeared to him on the road to Damascus, striking him blind. But my heart said the time was not yet come.

"It was Esther who answered. 'You must eat,' she said."

That is how my Sarkate friend Judah tells the tale, although I retain no data of that time, up until I asked what had happened to me. I see no reason to doubt any of the data Judah has given me.

Judah places warm, wet applications upon the area of my head he calls my eyes. When they become too dry or too cool, he removes them, and soon after reapplies them, warm and wet once more. There is pain in the mid-section of the corpus I inhabit, and Esther insists that "eating," the ingestion of physical matter to which I earlier alluded, will alleviate the discomfort. But I cannot bring myself to do so, yet. The very idea repulses me in ways I cannot explain to you who are without bodies, or to myself who wears a new one. Perhaps I will learn to overmaster my abhorrence. I shall try before dictating my next epistle. Esther says that the "wounds of my soul" are my own business, but that my physical well-being is, for now, her business. The wife of Judah is very insistent.

Yours from among the Sarkate,
Paul of Tarsus

—4—

SENT BY: Lillian.Uberland@rsi.edu

RECEIVED BY: MNA@sellenville.edu

Kiss-Kiss, Cousin!

And kick-kick, while I'm at it. Why did you even mention your issues with the Fundamentalist kids in Biology class? Why do I bother giving you advice? I get the impression you take every warning I give you and compile it into a personal To Do list. Stop being such a jarhead, Mikey!

But no, no, you've gotta be the great Apostle of Evolution. You're gonna clear the scales from the eyes of the masses, and make them see the glory and wonder of science. Hallelujah!

Obviously it's high time for me to write you fully on the painful subject of Reality. Sweetie, this is your first year of public school teaching. Does the word "tenure" mean anything to you? If you behave yourself for three years, just three, you'll be set for life. Compare that to the university tenure track I'm on at RSI, and you'll see you've landed the better deal . . . no pressures to publish, no frets that you'll perish.

All right, let's handle things from here, since there's no going back. You gave the class a unit test focused strictly, entirely, one hundred percent on evolution. You told them the test was coming; you reviewed all the materials for three days in advance; and at the end of the testing class, your seven Fundie students handed in pages that were completely blank.

Little cousin, you've now planted your butt firmly on the head of the bull and grabbed yourself a dilemma by both horns. Here are your options, and each one could pretty much impale you.

First: flunk the little connivers. No one in the school's administration can say you have insufficient grounds. For one, they failed the test, plain and simple, and they earned zero out of one hundred points being offered that day in your classroom. And two, they deliberately, consciously chose to sacrifice those points so that they could make *their* point. Great big "F's" all around, point made, have a nice day.

But taking that road leads exactly where I said you don't want to go. You capture the attention of their parents, and you turn your Biology course into an "issue." Even that wouldn't be so bad, except that your last email told me something that puts the situation in an even harsher light: the seven students all belong to the same church. That, kiddo, is a very bad thing. You see, if one of them attended Elm Street Church of Christ, another attended Word of the Savior Chapel, a third attended Mount Whatever Evangelical Congregation and so on, you could easily divide and conquer the parent battalion. The reason Fundies have so many churches . . . churches that are almost indistinguishable to you and me, as far as their beliefs go . . . is because these people will sink their teeth in and fight about *anything* they consider to be an important issue. Is the King James Version the only acceptable translation of the Bible, or is the Revised Standard Version okay? They argue about it, dig in, and a group breaks off to start a new Fundamentalist church. Will Jesus save Christians before the Great Tribulation of their prophesied End Times, or will he wait until after? Out pops a new splinter congregation. Should kids be allowed to attend school dances, or is that immodest and unholy? Another argument, another schism.

As a group, Fundies are united only in their ability to be absolutely right, whatever the cost, at every given moment. No matter what it does to them as a group.

But you're not lucky enough to be dealing with that. You'll be dealing with fourteen parents who fellowship with one another every Sunday morning and each Wednesday and Friday evening. They pray together. They raise their children together. They vote as a bloc in elections. And they'll swarm, a single-minded mob, into your principal's office, insist in one voice that you are promoting Satanism, and demand you be fired without further discussion.

The principal, being a reasonable man who knows all about Supreme Court decisions banning the teaching of Creationism in public school science classes, will try to placate them. He'll say how much he sympathizes with their position, but that the law of the land directs that all religious instructions about Adam and Eve, seven days of creation, and a talking snake need to take place outside the school day.

But he'll have never known the likes of the pressure these fourteen parents can wield as a group. One of them will raise the point that evolution is itself a religious issue, since it promotes an anti-God view of the world that their religion finds repugnant. Another will throw in that the children are having their freedom of expression repressed, since what they were really doing by handing in blank tests was protesting the guidance of an evil, atheistic Biology teacher (that's you, Mikey). A third will complain that the kids' grade-point averages shouldn't be harmed just because they're Christian, and then that parent will use the word "persecution."

That's when the first crack will appear, because the last thing your principal, decent man that he is, wants to see in the daily *Sellenville Post* is the headline, "Kids Flunked For Being Christian, Parents Charge." His high school does not need that kind of press coverage. So he'll make the offer. He'll say that he'll go and talk to you, Mikey sweet, to see what you can "do about those grades." He'll mention the possibility of an alternate assignment.

Then the group will see that crack in your principal's defenses, and they'll step back. From them will emerge the one they silently acknowledge as their true leader. He's the Alpha Fundie. In your last email, you mentioned the mousy, stringy-haired girl, the one in the Fundie group who's so quiet and who never really challenges you directly. My money says that her father's the Alpha. The way you describe her, she shows all the signs of growing up in a very strict, very regimented home. The kind where "Honor thy father and thy mother" is exactly as important as "Thou shalt not kill," and where the belt rack is adorned with a Bible-verse sign declaring, "He that spareth his rod hateth his son."

Alpha Fundie says to your principal: "Creationism *is* science." And he'll start talking, sounding far more scientifically knowledgeable than your principal expects. He'll use the line about evolution only being a "theory." Then he'll bring up the topics of mutations and probability, and he may even pull out a pen and paper to show the mathematics that prove, yes *prove*, that the likelihood of primordial ooze mutating into something as complex as a human being is equal to the likelihood of an explosion in a print shop blowing metal printing letters everywhere that, by mere chance, land on the ground and spell out the complete works of Shakespeare, flawlessly.

Alpha Fundie will use this analogy even though most printing today is done digitally, without those metal letters.

By now your principal is flustered. As bright as he is, he'll have gotten lost in all the pseudo-scientific babble. In his confused state, he'll come away with just one tangible idea: that his Biology teacher is kind of a troublemaker.

His *untenured* Biology teacher.

I mentioned at the start of this (now way-too-long) email that it was a dilemma you face. The first horn was flunking the kids and dealing with everything above. Luckily, the second horn is far quicker to cover: disregard the tests. Tell the students you're not counting their zeros. Send home notes to the parents as well. They'll feel the brief thrill of victory, and then happily go on with their lives without you as an "issue."

Of course, this means you have to violate everything you hold dear about both education and science. But I say go for it. Spare them the science. You're young. You have plenty of time for idealism once you're tenured. After that, go nuts, and your Teachers Union rep will do all the fighting for you. Union reps live for that sort of thing.

Put this one to rest, Mikey love. If you get run out of town by believers, I'd feel obligated to let you stay with me, and I've only got one bedroom.

Your affectionate cousin,
Doctor Lillian

—5—

Greetings to my kind, the No-Flesh Asarkos,

It would seem that the king for whom I work, Herod Agrippa, is a very evil Sarkate. At least that is the assurance I get from Esther, wife of Judah, who has spoken with me much more than she did during my first few days here. Herod Agrippa apparently joined in an illicit liaison with his own cousin, a custom forbidden here. He also feuds with his uncle, another king who is also named Herod (except he, the second, is properly called Herod Antipas). Both King Herods play an endless game of trying to have the other accused of treason against the third king, Gaius Caesar, and Herod Agrippa, for whom I work, has an advantage due to his early friendship with Gaius, also called Caligula.

"No," Judah said gently to his wife, "it is Herod Antipas who has joined in marriage illicitly with his own kin. It was not his cousin, it was his niece."

"And then he had her executed?" Esther asked.

"Not at all," Judah said. "You are confusing that with stories from your childhood. It was Herod the Great who had his wife executed, many years before you and I were born."

The sounds I always associate with Esther, the banging and clanging of items and elements I cannot envision, those sounds ceased. "Too many Herods, too many kings, and not enough righteousness in the land. It's all too confusing for a woman's mind."

Without expecting to, I burst forth with rushes of air and sound, released from what feels to be an internal chamber of this body. I felt strangely happy having done this, but then stopped, cautious about having made such an involuntary disturbance. I was reassured when I heard similar sounds coming from Judah and Esther.

"You have a good laugh," Esther said, "the laugh of a healthy man. Not of a monster."

"I do not know why I reacted that way," I told them. "I was struck with an odd resonation, hearing you speak aloud the very confusion and consternation I was weighing in my own thoughts. Herods and kings everywhere!" Again, I laughed.

More somber, Judah said, "There is only one king who matters, and that is the King of All."

"Amen," Esther said. I felt her touch my shoulder when she said that. Here in this epistle, I have told Judah to write that his companion and wife Esther is a fine Sarkate, and that I enjoy her friendship as much as I enjoy his.

I think, now, of The Ten Who Are Missing, the ones whom I seek as part of this mission I am on. It strikes me that they may have fallen into the waves of Our Enemies, and that they are no longer in existence. That makes me sad, for among them were several I enjoyed as friends. I wish I could explain to Judah a way to record their emanations in this epistle, for I, unlike the Sarkate, have no names by which to call The Ten, that I might write about them individually, and remember.

And now I think of the larger concern, the concern of the entire Asarkos race. I think of how the universe grows unendingly, and how we must work harder to maintain our very existence. One day the universe will grow too large, and the strength that sustains us will not be enough. First we will grow too weak to convey data to one another, and we will live for eons in the isolation of broken communication. Which of us knows what sort of madness such aloneness will inflict on our sentience? And then, much later, when the universe stretches us beyond the trillion-raised-by-a-trillion cubits we know to be the outer limits of our sustainability, then the end shall come. We will be no more. The aims of Our Enemies will be achieved, a gift handed to them by the universe itself. We can no longer believe that we are going to live forever. It is appointed unto us a time to die.

We have existed since the universe began. We have been self-aware for a quarter of that time. We have been fully sentient for but a quarter of that quarter, and have grown among the forces and energies and waves of the heavens, gathering new information slowly, always too slowly. What sadness that at the pinnacle of our self-understanding, we should learn the truth: the universe that gave us life must soon take it back. We were its firstborn, in whom a single wavelength can stretch from star to star . . . but the future belongs to the shorter waves, like Our Enemies. Or perhaps like these matter sentients, of whom I am becoming very fond. Perhaps they, and not Our Enemies, are the future.

"This King of All Kings," I said to Judah and Esther. "He is the one I would most like to meet."

They said nothing for a time.

"Is he unavailable to meet with me?" I asked, for I was trying to understand their silence.

"He died," Judah said slowly, "and then he came to life again, raised by the hand of God. He ascended into heaven, five years ago. But he returned once more, appearing to you on the road to Damascus. He filled you with his holy spirit, and you cried out in the languages of many nations, and in the tongues of angels as well."

I told Judah that I wished I could remember that. I asked him to tell me everything he knew about the Risen Christ, the King of All Kings, and Judah became very excited at my interest. He wishes to go away and return with a Sarkate called Ananias, who can tell me all about the Risen Christ. He wished to leave immediately to summon Ananias, but I begged his patience, requesting that he first write all of this epistle. I will stop now. Judah is very anxious to fetch this other Sarkate, and it would be most unkind to this kind man should I keep him any longer. In my next epistle, we will record what I learned of the Risen Christ.

Yours from among the Sarkate,
Paul of Tarsus

—6—

SENT BY: Lillian.Uberland@rsi.edu
RECEIVED BY: MNA@sellenville.edu

Kiss-Kiss, Cousin,

Are you completely nuts, sweetie?

I suppose you think your new approach to the Creationist situation is clever and unexpected. Well, it's certainly unexpected, that I'll give you. But I regret missing the day you got your frontal lobotomy. Please tell me that a lobotomy *is* what happened; I can't think of any other explanation for your brain turning off the way it has.

Mikey, I appreciate your desire to challenge the situation head-on, but holding a "Creationist Day" in your Biology class is the worst possible approach . . . especially sending the Fundamentalist parents an invitation to provide their own guest speaker. Don't get ahead of me here, I know exactly what you're thinking. You're closing your eyes and imagining your-self up in front of your classes, going head to head with some Bible-wav-ing bumpkin who claims God created light on the first day of creation. That first day of creation, he asserts, took place a mere 10,000 years ago. When the bumpkin is done spouting, you'll raise your oh-so-scientific finger and say, "Aha! You've just claimed that light was created on the first day! However, your own Bible says that the sun and stars were not created until the *fourth* day! And since light, by definition, is the emission of photons from stars (here you'll point out that the sun is itself just another star, something the infallible writer of Genesis seems to have missed), then the Bible claims star *emissions* started several days *before* stars were around to emit them! How do you deal with *that*, Mr. Bumpkin?"

Oh, how Mr. Bumpkin fumes and sputters in your little fantasy. He shakes his Bible at you and yells, "The Word of God cannot be in error! God made light, and then he made the Earth and sky on the next day! The day after that he made the ground bring forth all vegetation and plants and trees, and a day later he made the heavenly bodies that shine on the Earth! On the fifth day God brought forth the fish of the seas, the birds of the air, and the cattle, wild beasts, and creeping things of the land. Amen and verily, I say, God then, on the sixth day, created man and woman in His own image and likeness! And on the seventh day, He rested!"

You're smiling patiently through all this, letting him blow off steam, giving him his one minute of not-so-glorious say-so. Because your trap is set. You nod, indicating how tolerant you're being; you sweep back your hair with one hand in that way I've always thought is so cute; and then you level him. "Bumpkin, old man," you say, "those plants you created on the third day are in deep trouble. They've got to spend twenty-four hours sitting on a rock called Earth in the middle of a sunless, heatless universe. Even granting you a little light for photosynthesis from your first-day's magic trick with photons, you've still got major problems. Your plants are frozen to crystal the second they're created, just a surely as if you'd dunked them all in liquid nitrogen. When the fourth day hits, they'll shatter at the first wave of warmth that comes crashing down from your spanking-new sun. And when the fifth day arrives, the animals you made will have nothing to eat. You've just given us the recipe for building a lifeless planet."

The class sits in stunned silence as realization of your brilliance sinks in. Then they begin to laugh, a laughter born of sheer joy at your unassailable logic . . . their teacher, going toe-to-toe with the Voice of God, and humbling God's own spokesman, Mr. Bumpkin. They'll hoot for you, applaud a little, some may even taunt poor Bumpkin (you'll gently correct them, of course; gloating is unnecessary, since the joy of Science and Reason is its own reward). By the end of the class period, Bumpkin will still be sputtering and making silly claims about Noah hiking all the way to Australia to fetch male and female koala bears, but your students . . . your disciples! . . . will have tuned him out, awash in a new-found respect for the truths you've unveiled. The scales have fallen from their eyes. Each of them is a future scientist. Each of them is a mini-Mikey. As they depart from class, the quiet, mousy girl you always mention will look up at you and whisper in her mousy way, "Gosh. You're really smart."

That would be fun, wouldn't it? Even I had fun writing it. Bad news, though. It's time to shut down the Creationist conquest fantasy, Mikey love. 'Cause it ain't gonna happen that way. I'll tell you what will really go down.

But first, since I brought it up, a short aside on Mousy Girl. I never would have been so callous in my ranting about her imaginary father as the Alpha Fundie, had I known that her father died last year. That's awful, and I'm sorry I said what I did. You sounded a little pissed at me for the gaffe, and you're obviously very fond of her. Mikey, my heart, please believe that I was only playing around, and that when I spin my imaginary scenarios, it's only to make my point. In the light of cold, hard reality, I would never be so unfeeling, never.

So back to cold, hard reality. The Bumpkin Creationist in your fantasy hasn't been active since the mid-1900s. Sure, those folks are still around, the types who proudly display their neural stagnation by proclaiming, "God's Word says it, I believe it, that settles it." But that won't be who shows up at your classroom door on Creationism Day. And now it won't be a local Alpha Fundie, either, since you've opened the door to let the church parents invite a "guest speaker." You've guaranteed yourself a visit from an out-of-towner Creation Scientist. Let's call him Doctor Hired Gun.

Yes, cousin, Creationists have doctors in their ranks. Never mind that his Ph.D. is in sociology, you'll still need to introduce him to your Biology class as Doctor Hired Gun, and any qualifiers you add to that "doctor" title will be lost on a bunch of tenth graders. This man is an Authority, and you're just Mr. Mike, public school teacher from Sellenville.

Doctor Gun stands for his presentation. Funny, he doesn't have a Bible in his hand. What's that he's carrying? Why, it's a copy of Charles Darwin's *On the Origin of Species By Means Of Natural Selection,* the very book that started all this crazy talk about evolution—a book you wrote a term paper on once, but which Doctor Gun has read, re-read, scrutinized, analyzed, and put under Jehovah's microscope. He can quote from that book, chapter and page, as easily as he can quote from the Holy Scriptures. He'd love you to test him on that. That's why he's carrying it; not for the kids, but for you.

Doctor Gun starts talking, but he's not saying anything about the six days of creation. Even weirder, he's not talking about Darwin, either. The first thing he says after his pleasantries and self-introductions is, "Kids, I'd like to teach you about the Second Law of Thermodynamics, and how that Law contradicts the claims made by the theory of evolution."

Dizzy yet? This sociologist Fundamentalist is waving around evolution literature and spouting laws from physics instead of biology. (To save you from rummaging through old notebooks to find your scribblings on it from General Science 101, the Second Law of Thermodynamics is this: the entropy of a closed system never decreases, and increases whenever possible. In simpler terms: stuff don't build up, it breaks down.)

Doctor Gun will explain this Law to your students, and he'll make it very interesting. He's a better speaker than you are, he's more entertaining, his jokes are perfect for the age group. He may even throw in some clever supporting lyrics from songs on the Top-Ten-Charts-of-Coolest-Music-This-Week-for-Fifteen-Year-Olds. Ironically, your seven Fundamentalist students won't catch the lyric references, since they're not allowed to listen to the devil's music. But the rest will. And they'll be happy to learn, in nice, simple, fifteen-year-old terms, that the universe follows a Law that makes everything tend toward entropy, sheer breakdown.

And they'll, like, you know, really relate, 'cause every fifteen-year-old already feels like life sucks, and it's, you know, falling apart.

While they chew on that, Doctor Gun reaches into his satchel, and out pop the visual aids: a great big glossy photo of a parakeet with more splashes of dramatic color than Joseph's multi-colored dream coat; next to it: a second photo, a big black-and-white microscope shot of an amoeba. "Evolutionists *believe*," Doctor Gun says, "that their *theory* explains how this single-celled organism grew up to become this marvelous bird. It kept reproducing, and changing, and reproducing, and changing, and we wound up with a very complex flying creature. But what does the *law* of thermodynamics tell us?"

That stuff breaks down, your kids tell him.

"Yes, especially over long periods of time," says Doctor Gun. "Metal rusts, ice cream melts, stars burn out. What wouldn't break down, given enough time? But here comes Charles Darwin, trying to tell you just the opposite . . . with a *theory* that tries to reverse what scientists themselves call a *law*, the Second Law of Thermodynamics."

"Wait a minute!" you protest, holding up that oh-so-scientific finger again, but wagging it with a little less confidence. "The Second Law of Thermodynamics only applies to *closed* systems. The Earth isn't a closed system. It receives energy from the sun."

Doctor Gun smiles at the class, showing how tolerant he is of your misunderstanding. "But the universe *is* a closed system. And when we talk about life 'evolving,' we're talking about that happening in the *universe*, aren't we? Unless you think we live somewhere else."

The class chuckles. At you.

"No," you say, "but the Earth is an open system and has energy pouring into it, so it's an exception to the rule."

"You're saying that Earth is an exception to the Second Law of Thermodynamics?"

"No," you sputter, "I'm saying it's not an example of what you're talking about. Otherwise, *nothing* would ever become more complex. Simple drops of water in the air wouldn't be able to turn into complex snowflakes."

Doctor Gun looks surprised, and turns to the class so they'll see his stunned expression. "Are you saying that a *snowflake* is as important, is on the same level, as the creation of *life?*"

You can see that he's moved on to word games. He isn't doing "science," not any more than you and I were doing "medicine" when we were kids playing doctor. But you're trapped. There's no way out of the Creationist downward spiral. "All right, then, I'll use a different example. A baby developing in the womb. If the Second Law of Thermodynamics says that things *always* break down, then there's no way that a baby could develop. It would violate your interpretation of the Law."

"Or perhaps," Doctor Gun says . . . with his eyes, he signals the class to get ready for a little more levity . . . "it won't turn out to be a baby at all. Given an evolutionist's beliefs, it could very well come out a monkey!" He laughs along with the class. "That's what evolutionists call 'mutation,'" he tells them, "and in *theory* it's a good thing. But don't worry, I'm not an evolutionist. I won't be calling you a bunch of mutants."

Then he tosses out a mini-lesson on mutations, and gives the class an intro to probability, convincing them that the spontaneous evolution of beneficial mutations is mind bogglingly unlikely. You counter with arguments about natural selection having billions of years to occur. He whips through a couple of convincing explanations about how scientists don't really know the age of the Earth, and that Mr. Mike has a *belief* about the Earth's age, not a fact. And you counter that. Then he counters you. You argue back. He argues forth.

The class stopped paying close attention ten minutes ago. You think you've proved your point, but the victory goes to Doctor Gun for one simple reason: he's convinced them that maybe he could be right, too. Even the ones who don't believe him will conclude that he's made some pretty good arguments. They couldn't repeat those arguments, of course, but they'll always remember that you had to work hard to try to prove Doctor Hired Gun wrong.

And that gives him his victory. Because your out-of-towner Creation Scientist doesn't have to show that his ideas are right, he just has to show that a lot of yours *could* be wrong. He never expected to win. He just needed a draw. That's because he's counting on the knee-jerk reaction that if evolution is disproved, the only other option is Creationism. He knew the kids would get tired of the scientific details, so he only had to create uncertainty, so that their minds would be filled with contradictory pictures.

And where science leaves off, democracy steps in. "We've had a great discussion about what evolutionists believe versus what Creationists believe," Doctor Gun will say in his summary. "Your teacher's been great! He's been very convincing in some of his points, and I hope a lot of mine have been convincing, too. If you've learned anything today, I hope it's that your science classes have room for both Creationist and evolutionist beliefs, so that you'll be able to decide for yourselves what's true. Your teacher has taken an important step toward making science education more fair."

It's only fair. More than any other specimen of *Homo sapiens,* the fifteen-year-old understands and cherishes that sweepingly democratic phrase. *Decide for yourselves what's true.* Even a school board would nod agreeably at that one, until you pointed out that no one in Math class is rewarded for having faith that 2+2=5. *Your teacher's been great.* Go ahead, contradict that. Tell them, "Nah, I've been a twit."

Mikey love, do you know what I did today? I taught a basic lesson in cellular structure to a bunch of college freshmen, proctored a Macro exam for Doctor Kairns, and made a little more headway in the fly lab, confirming the genetic influences on ocular structure for *Drosophila*—fruit fly eyeball genes, something we've had mapped for years, but which we review and re-review and then check again, because that's what biology is all about. As tedious as it is, we know that not one little *Drosophila* allele will get by us. If we fight, it's among ourselves, not with those who reject science wholesale. There's more honor in battling a worthy opponent.

More safety, too.

I'd tell you to back out of the Creationist Day idea, but I'm afraid you'll go ahead with it just to spite me. So it'll have to suffice that I've pointed out the error of your ways. Choose well, kiddo.

Your affectionate cousin,
Doctor Lillian

−7−

Greetings to my kind, the No-Flesh Asarkos,

You cannot imagine. I cannot describe it. I must contain my excitement and speak slowly, so that Judah can record my words, no matter how jumbled they sound as they come from me.

I can see! And the colors! I can tell you what they are, and the fractions of wavelength cubits the color waves inhabit on the spectrum; I can tell you my suspicions about how the eyes of the Sarkate function, receiving the light waves and translating them to imagery in their minds so that their sentience can absorb and interpret them. I can give you all the details, but I have no power to communicate the experience. The colors!

They laugh for joy with me, the ones who have been here in the home of Judah and Esther for several days now. There is Ananias, the friend of Judah who has been telling me the story of the Risen Christ and His importance. There is Luke, a physician like Judah, a Greek man friendly to the followers of Christ, although not himself a follower. It was Luke and Judah who laid their hands upon me while Ananias prayed, and Luke who has been rubbing the herbal salve onto the scales that covered my eyes. Luke's voice was light and playful, even as he chided Judah for the treatments I had received.

"You covered his eyes with warm compresses?" Luke asked.

"Of course, I did," said Judah. "His head was feverish, so I moved to cure like with like."

"Like with like?" Luke sounded aghast. "Where on Earth did a Jewish physician learn such a thing?"

"From Greek physicians, as is happens."

I felt Luke checking the extremities called my hands and my feet. "There is your problem," Luke said to Judah. "The words of Hippocrates still pertain, four hundred years after he said them: that we Greeks have many who call themselves physicians, but few who truly are."

Judah asked Luke many questions about the salve they applied to the scales over my eyes, and seemed disappointed that it was made of oil from leaves on trees found far away from Damascus.

The encrustations loosened and fell. Even Luke gasped at how quickly the treatment worked! There they are on the floor now, broken free and lying in wondrous brown and gray and black crusted glory!

Brown, gray, black, those are colors, three colors from among thousands. And my friends, they too have colors, and I see them with depths that can only be compared with the nuances of electrolocation feedback absorbed from the deepest of projected fields. And my friends look as they ought to look, I sense them being the right shapes and sizes, because my brain, too, kindly makes sense of the light waves. As simple as that, the matter does the work for my sentience and awareness.

The glory of the Sarkate! The glory of the flesh, and of the generous gift of sight from these men, the friends of the Risen Christ!

Oh, I must calm myself.

———

It is later now. I have eaten and it did not repulse me, just as Esther, wife of Judah, promised. "Paul of Tarsus," she said to me, "God has worked a great miracle on you. You should keep your body strong, now that He has fully healed you."

It operates in this manner, as nearly as I can deduce: the Sarkate race, or to use one of their own words, "mankind," is constructed of highly organized matter particles. Groups of particles specialize into discreet organs that perform a variety of tasks. The hands are made for grasping other material objects and manipulating them. The feet give the body balance, acting as bases for long legs that allow the Sarkate to move from one place to another. The head is the home of thoughts and the seat of sentience, a single part that thinks for, and commands, the whole. Eyes in the head absorb waves of light, and ears attached to each side collect disturbances in the air, transforming noise and sound and the conversations of my friends into patterns my head can understand. The Sarkate have other organs, too, which they cover in a special act of dignity with cloths and layers of robing.

Judah has stopped writing just now. It seems I used a very inappropriate term for the other organs the Sarkate keep hidden under their clothes. The Sarkate do not discuss these openly, and I have violated one of their speaking codes.

"I cannot imagine any part of the body can be so disturbing," I said to Judah.

"There are some things that are unclean," Judah insisted.

"But you must consider them to be very important," I said, "because you treat them with care and special honor by covering them."

"We cover our members to hide them, not to honor them."

I spoke quite freely. "The first man Adam did not hide his members, for he was innocent of sin before eating from the tree of the knowledge of good and evil. You have told me that the Risen Christ has freed you from sin. If all sin is gone, are not all things permitted to you?"

Ananias, who was still in the room, stepped toward me. The Greek physician Luke was also still with us. He was smiling at me, and I could not help feeling I recognized him. I have told Judah to record this.

Ananias said, "Do my ears deceive me? Am I hearing the message of Christ from Saul of Tarsus, favorite student of the Pharisees? Are you really telling us that sin is conquered? What of our Law and our Prophets?"

"The Law is made for man, not man for the Law." I was quite animated in the way I spoke, and not entirely certain what I was saying. "If your Risen Christ has put sin to death, could it be he has put your Law to death as well?"

"This!" said Judah. "This is a kind of talk likely to get us killed!"

"You are still shocked from your injuries," Ananias said, more gently than Judah. "Christ has shown us how to be the people of God. He taught us that the Law is summed up in the commandments of love. The Law is love."

"And Christ is love," Judah said.

"And Christ has died," Luke said. He spoke little about the topic my friends call Religion, deferring to the other Sarkate. His skin was somewhat darker than theirs, and his clothing was far more elaborate and colorful. Judah and Ananias both had facial hair, as did I; Luke's skin was clear. Those and other subtle differences were my first clues that he belonged to a class of Sarkate known as "Gentiles."

"I'm following the extended syllogism our friend Saul has helped you build," Luke said. "Law equals love, Christ equals love, Christ equals dead, and so, the Law is dead."

Now Judah spoke with great ire. "We do not need the pagan logics of a Greek philosopher! You are a guest in my home!"

"And having me here is, I believe, a violation of your Hebrew Law." I was confused, because Luke seemed to be having a light and pithy conversation, while Judah was arguing with fervor.

"Letting you in my home is a different matter! With the turmoil in Damascus, I accept you because you are not against us!"

"Nor am I for you," Luke said. "So what does that mean?"

"That you will be spit out," I said. I did not say it to chide him, the words just came, feeling like words I had always known. Ananias and Judah looked surprised, but they could not have been as surprised as me.

It was then that I had the memory, and I have Judah record it here for me. I am a young man . . . not me, but Saul of Tarsus . . . and I am in Jerusalem. I am a student of the Pharisee Gamaliel, but I am also in the tutelage of Blastus, an associate of Herod Agrippa, not yet king. Luke and I . . . I, Saul, knew this Luke! . . . are listening to the words of Jesus of Nazareth, as he addresses his closest disciples and a growing band of followers. One of the things Jesus says is, "If you are not for me, you are against me." This strikes both Luke and me as strange, for the week previous he had told a crowd, "If you are not against me, you are for me." There would seem to be no middle ground. Luke and I joke that Jesus must treat his followers like hot or cold food; either temperature will do, but food that is lukewarm will be spit from the mouth of the master.

In the house of Judah, Luke drew near and laid a hand upon my shoulder.

"You will be spit out," I repeated. "It is a memory of mine."

"I know," Luke says. "Perhaps more will come."

"I remembered Adam was the first man. I have read that in the Law. I have read many things in the Law."

"Yes," said Luke, "and few knew the Hebrew Law as well as you. It may all come back to you, but you are different now." Luke smiles more than my other two Sarkate friends, and I think it is because he sees a humor in things that he rarely speaks aloud. "I think I, too, will henceforth call you Paul."

"He is Paul, the humbled one, because he has seen the Risen Christ." Ananias sounded very solemn again.

"Jesus of Nazareth!" I said, putting it together. "*He* is the Risen Christ! He is the King of All."

"You should be baptized in his name," Ananias said, and I agreed to that.

I have stolen this scroll from Judah. I have remembered how to write, and now I do so for myself. See how large my handwriting is? I cannot tell him everything I now think. My policy, for the moment, is to conceal myself.

The Sarkate have a very complex social structure, and they, like we, have enemies. Unlike us, their enemies are within the race, not apart from it. Sarkate have the power to deprive one another of life. Just as Our Enemies are waves that destroy other waves, so among this race are Sarkate made of flesh who destroy the flesh of others.

I do not know who are enemies and who are friends, and the interactions are such that I may put myself in danger. I do not like to deceive Judah, for I do count him as a friend. But I am Asarkos made flesh, and I do not understand my vulnerabilities. I have been baptized into their fellowship, for they say I have been born again in flesh and in spirit. It strikes me that they do not know how profoundly accurate that pronouncement is.

Luke seems to be my friend. But clearly he is not the friend of Judah, while I am friend to both. I must be wary. I do not know who I am for, or who I am against.

This scroll must remain private. Henceforth I shall carry it upon my person, at all times.

Yours from among the Sarkate,
Paul of Tarsus

—8—

SENT BY: Lillian.Uberland@rsi.edu
RECEIVED BY: MNA@sellenville.edu

Kiss-Kiss, Cousin,

This week started out fantastic! While checking up on my latest batch of force-bred *Drosophila melanogaster* . . . fruit flies are my life, you know . . . I found that my post-larval winged friends had failed to mutate as I planned. I thought I was taking a healthy population of black-eyes, breeding out portions of the PAX6 gene, and creating a *sine oculis* condition. That means they'd be eyeless, a little like the rare aniridia condition in humans, congenital absence of the iris in an otherwise healthy baby. Well, either I didn't follow the process or my flies didn't follow the rules. The next generation developed massive (for them) growths entirely covering their eyes. Some extreme cases of the matting grew twice as large as the eyes themselves, like a mega-severe case of ulcerative blepharitis in human eyes. One small difference: blepharitis isn't lethal in humans. Nearly every fruit fly of that generation, on the other hand, is resting in eternal peace, dead little dots at the bottom of their bell jars.

Not all of them gave up the ghost. The six percent of *Drosophila* that didn't succumb to their own brand of blepharitis tended to exhibit direct ocular malformations, developing half again the number of facets found in a typical compound eye. That might have a correlation in humans, too: mis-positioned pupils, *ectopia pupillae,* although each of our eyes has only a single pupil to be mis-positioned. There my insights end, since I'm no medical doctor.

So I'm thinking, "This is way cool, I have to reduplicate the alteration!" and I write up a quick summary, no longer than an abstract, for Doctor Kairns. That was yesterday; this morning he walks into my office, and I'm ready to hear something like, "Lillian, this is intriguing. You might be on to something big here. Can we start a proposal for getting you a whole bunch of grant money?"

You see, little Cousin? Like you, I make the mistake of falling into fantasies. Because what Doctor Kairns really said when he walked in was: "Why is a member of our department advising a public-school Biology teacher to handle Creationists by 'sparing them the science'?"

I didn't know what he meant at first. Then I remembered using that line in an email to you. I flushed with paranoia: was Doctor Kairns reading my emails? Would the university allow that level of invasion into my privacy? They could do it by law, but would they really *do* it?

Had things only been that benign. Doctor Kairns handed me the morning paper, and there I was, being quoted by you in an article headlined, "God Gets Invited Back to School." Subhead: "Local science teacher to sponsor Creationism Day at Sellenville High." And paragraph 6: "'Open dialogue is important to science, to society, and to education,' said Biology teacher Michael N. Atkins. 'My own cousin, a scientist, advised me to handle my Creationist students by sparing them the science. But I think my approach opens more doors to discussion and harmony between schools and local faith communities.'"

Oh, and lest I be sheltered under any cloaks of anonymity, there was the follow-up in the next paragraph: "Atkins's cousin, Doctor Lillian Uberland, is a professor of Biology at RSI."

Thanks for the plug, Cuz. I won't bore you with details of the upbraiding I got from Kairns. I won't mention how long I stewed until I could finally talk without sputtering. But I will share this: for today at least, I don't love you anymore.

Still, I do see the bright side. There, in the same article, your principal (*your* boss, *your* evaluator for tenure) is quoted as praising your innovation and ingenuity. I'm very proud of you for that political score. But I admit I considered taking back all the nice things I assumed about your principal a few emails ago. If the man doesn't realize that this is a backdoor you've opened for a religious fringe movement . . . an opening that violates the spirit, if not the letter, of Supreme Court decisions on teaching Creationism in public schools . . . then he's not as informed an administrator as I'd imagined. But I don't want to be too quick on the draw here. Perhaps he was blindsided the way I was; perhaps he, too, was put on the spot by your chatting to the press about Creationism Day.

Mikey love, why do you and I always go through times like this? We grow close to one another, we fall back, we reconcile, we find a reason to argue and break apart again. It's as if our nearest approach to constancy is endless undulation, back, forth, back, forth. We shouldn't be like that! We're about the only stable things to come from Grandma and Grandpa's gene pool, and we were always able to stay detached from most of the family hysteria. We promised each other we'd always be above that. But we find ourselves falling back into the old one-upsmanship patterns our families suffered.

I remember visiting you during your first year of college. I was starting my post-grad coursework, you were just sticking your toe into the waters of Science for Grownups. That night we lay on the hill behind your dorm, looking at the stars, holding hands and talking about all our plans, everything we'd do with our lives now that we'd moved beyond those all-but-dysfunctional families of ours. We saw two shooting stars, and you said cosmology was your calling. I was entrenched in my fruit flies, and I knew even then that I'd never want to move far beyond them and their four measly chromosomes. And you, my little Cousin and friend, you swore we'd work together to take the science world by storm. I chided you, told you cosmology and genetics were different worlds. I said we'd never find a project that covered them both. You disagreed. You made an oath that together we'd work to find a Theory of Everything.

And here we are today. You've abandoned the stars and are teaching in my field (mine, mine, mine, you brat), and I'm sending you long email treatises on the nature of the universe and how the world was formed . . . far more like cosmology than I thought I'd ever have to deal with. We didn't create our Theory of Everything, Mikey. We just stumbled across it, unaware, and its name is Creationism. Just ask the holy elect, when they swarm into your classroom next week, and they'll tell you. They have One Theory, and it accounts for anything you can imagine.

You made me mad by quoting me out of context, Mikey. By quoting me so publicly, and for putting me at risk with my own tenure review committee. You know me, and you know that's not the sort of thing I take lying down; I come from the same one-upsmanship gene pool as you. So no matter how much I love you, it's almost a biological imperative that I respond in kind.

"Dialogue," you emphasized in your newspaper interview. Funny, I don't see it as "dialogue" when you give Creationists a full, unchallenged day at your chalk board. "Opening more doors to discussion," you told the press, yet your Creationism Day is to be a one-sided monologue by a Creation "scientist." Wouldn't it be more useful to have a professional there to rebut false claims? Not a professional *educator*, but a real-life professional scientist. That would make it a real dialogue, don't you agree?

Actually, it doesn't matter whether you agree. Your principal already has. He's calling you tomorrow to let you know.

Mikey, he was thrilled to hear directly from the only person referenced in your article who had the nerve to suggest that all this might be a *bad* idea for a science class. And he was tickled pink to learn that I'd be happy to make time in my busy schedule to represent the forces of reason in your classroom. Creationist Day is no longer a monologue, Cousin. It's a debate.

I look forward to meeting the enemy on your turf. It'll be great fun!

Your affectionate cousin,
Doctor Lillian

—9—

Greetings to my kind, the No-Flesh Asarkos,

Today, as for the last four days, Ananias taught me of the Risen Christ. I am a master of the Torah and the Prophets, but Ananias moves through the sacred Scriptures of the Hebrews with a speed not unlike a startled gazelle. He points out references to Jesus of Nazareth in the writings of the prophet Isaiah, centuries before Jesus was born. He cites evidence for him in Moses' Genesis writings. For Ananias, Jesus is the great lover in Solomon's Songs, the glorious Coming of the Day of the Lord in the prophet Joel, the rejected block that became the cornerstone praised in King David's Psalms. All of these references are familiar to me. All of them are new. The data . . . the memories . . . of Saul of Tarsus are accessible, but they elude me often in a way I now understand to be very Sarkate, very human. I know Saul of Tarsus, but I must work hard to know that I know him. I see him dimly, as if he were but a poor reflection in a Sarkate glass.

While Ananias deluged me with data on the Christ, Luke and Judah argued about medicine. Today's argument (they have one every day, beginning shortly after sunrise and ending just after dinner) was about the efficacy of prayer as a supplement to the efficacy of poultices. Judah insisted that no ointment should be applied to a patient without a proper invocation of the God of Israel. Luke, ever patronizing, asked why the God of Israel would create a medicine that could not work on its own.

"To His Greater glory, the God of Israel requires that we remember Him in all the benefits He has given us!" Judah has sounded angry since the day I received my sight. I think he is an argumentative Sarkate, much of the time. "We invoke the Lord because all things, including medicines, are His good gifts."

"I see," said Luke. "Why, then, would God provide medicines at all? Why not simply give us invocations, that we might be healed directly by prayer?"

"God made the medicines to deliver healing to us!"

"Yet you say they do not work correctly if we do not pray."

"That is so."

"Then we have a mystery," Luke said. "For without the invocation, the medicine is useless, indicating that your God has created a gift which is an imperfect solution to sickness. Yet without the medicine, the invocation does little, for your God requires the use of the medicine, that medicine being the gift He offers for the purpose of healing. You create for me the picture of a God who is both imperfect and inefficient in his acts of creation."

"Pagan!" Judah cried in disgust. "You . . . disciple of Socrates!" It was Judah's most damning epithet. The argument would now fall silent for an hour.

Medicine. The Sarkate use it to prolong their existence. It came as a shock to me when I realized . . . remembered . . . how short the existence of a Sarkate is. In far less time than it takes light to travel from the core of one galaxy to another, a Sarkate comes into existence, grows to maturity, acquires knowledge at a rate surpassing, to an unthinkable degree, our most adept Asarkos data gatherers, and then withers and returns to particles of dust. You, my Asarkos brethren, must wonder why, then, they have not disappeared as a race, just as we ourselves are disappearing. Ah, there is the beauty of matter-made sentients. They simply make more copies of themselves. Not exact copies, but derivative offshoots. They do what we cannot: they create other sentients to replace themselves.

According to what we Asarkos know, there were 144 billion of us at the beginning of the universe. That number remained constant throughout the expansion of the cosmos. Then, during the last macrocosmic cycle, Our Enemies began to appear. Of course, we did not call them that at first. They were simply The Others, a second sentient race of waves. Our best thinkers, the forgers of our sciences, inferred their arrival into the universe through limited-frequency electrolocation probes. Then the wonder and bewilderment: the determination that the movements and activities of The Others were nonrandom, organized, intelligent.

What hope that gave us! The news traveled slowly through our race, as data always have. When the majority of us knew about the existence of The Others, the decision was made: we must befriend them, share information, learn about their nature that we might understand better not only them, but ourselves. Prior to knowing that The Others shared our universe, we did not realize how alone we were. In retrospect, we felt it, and still feel it today. Odd, that revelation. We did not know what it meant to be alone until knowledge of the universe told us, "You are not alone."

It took us a great deal of time, by time standards we did not then appreciate, to decide how best to approach The Others. And in that span, more than seven billion of us ceased to exist. Those seven billion Asarkos had encountered The Others, either by accident or out of curiosity, independently investigating the new form of sentient energy.

Over fifteen billion of us were gone by the time our sharing of data informed us that something was amiss.

Over thirty billion had been lost when we determined that The Others, although waves like ourselves, annulled our existence simply by interacting with us.

"Waves cannot cancel waves!" our best thinkers insisted, but even they withdrew their objections when the toll passed forty billion.

That was the beginning of the new despair. It was those events which led to our rules of non-engagement with The Others . . . Our Enemies . . .

and it was at that time our sciences reoriented toward the unthinkable subject of our own termination. We learned we are not naturally eternal, and that we as a race had a time limit correlated with the expansion of the universe. The knowledge of our impending end never would have come to us, had we not encountered Our Enemies. Through their new life, we found our death.

So what shall we expect of this third race, more unlike us even than Our Enemies? They absorb data quickly . . . so quickly, in fact, that their perspectives and interpretations of reality are constantly in conflict, as Luke and Judah clearly display. They work not only with data, but with suppositions and fanciful imaginings. They move from one argument to the next, tirelessly. Our race can point to times of disagreement and speak of them as eras: the Era in which we disagreed about the nature of Our Enemies; the Era in which we debated the time limits of our existence. But the Sarkate can cover those topics and more in the time it takes to eat a meal. I, too, now think that quickly, thanks to the flesh and mind of Saul of Tarsus. It occurs to me that the few letters I have written so far will take you the equivalent of a Sarkate lifetime to absorb.

What wondrous things are the Sarkate! A brief flicker in the span of time, yet able to hold almost as many data as any one of us. There are other creatures here upon the face of the Earth, thriving upon this small planet, yet none of them is as intelligent and capable as the being Man. The sheep grazes dumbly, dependent on Man for protection against the predator. The ass and the camel carry Man's belongings, sometimes rebellious but always subservient in the end. The wheat grows thoughtless in the field, showing no defense against Man's harvest and consumption. The bear of the mountain could easily kill a single Man, yet hides from him, as if aware that he has met his better. All living matter on this world forms a single, unbroken chain, from grass to tree to sheep to bear, and Man is the paragon of them all, He is the master and the measure, and if he but had a longer span of life, in knowledge he would be our better.

Esther came in from the outside and announced a new visitor. "A man has come, and he asks to speak with our guest Paul of Tarsus. He asks for him by the name 'Saul.'"

Judah looked concerned. "A man just walked up and spoke with you?"

"He is a Roman," Esther said, and that was sufficient explanation. The Jews are quite controlled in the interactions of their males and females. This has to do with the private parts of their bodies they go to great lengths to keep hidden. Roman Sarkate, on the other hand, are far freer with their interactions between the genders.

"Tell him Saul is still ill," Judah commanded.

"He knows that he is not, husband."

Ananias and Judah both looked at Luke, whose countenance hinted at surprised guilt. "I may have mentioned something at market. To an acquaintance, a friend who is a soldier."

"I would like to go outside," I said. In ten days and nights, I had not left the confines of Judah's home, learning about this world through the words of my friends and the memories of Saul. There had been so much to absorb, I never felt the need to exit the home. But word of a visitor, someone from beyond these walls, awakened in me a need for open air and direct sunlight.

"It's my fault," Luke said. He stood and walked toward the front room of the dwelling. "I'll put him off." It seemed no one had taken seriously my request to go outside, not even Saul's longest-time friend, Luke.

Luke was already through the outer door, so I barely whispered my repeat of the request, "I would like to go outside."

The men did not hear. Esther drew near to me, and set her hand on my face, the same way she did on the day she decided I was not a monster. "You shall go outside, friend Paul. Tomorrow I will nag my husband to let you outdoors."

My reaction to the touch was extreme. My pulse raced, and roiling overtook my stomach. And then there was the stirring of my most private member, the word for which is not spoken or written, as a matter of custom.

"Yes, tomorrow," I said hurriedly, for the memories of Saul railed against me, condemning me for the natural, yet unholy, responses of my Sarkate flesh.

Luke's normally dark complexion had paled when he returned indoors. "I have put him off for a time. It was not the one to whom I spoke, the simple soldier from the marketplace."

Judah . . . antagonist to Luke, but at heart a compassionate follower of the Risen Christ . . . pulled a bench from the back wall and kindly guided Luke to sit. Judah waved to Esther, who scooped spiced wine into a bowl for the ashen, frightened Greek doctor.

"Blastus," Luke said when he had swallowed some wine. "It was Blastus, courtier and advisor of King Herod Agrippa."

Too many kings, too many Herods. But with the mind of Saul at my command, I was no longer befuddled. For here was a secret I had kept even from my companion Luke: that I knew this Blastus well, and that I, too, was an advisor and counselor of Herod Agrippa, king over Palestine, tetrarch of Galilee, Perea, and other regions of Syria, a king who was himself a friend and advisor to Gaius Caligula Caesar.

This was a secret I needed to keep to myself, the memories of Saul informed me. The information would profoundly concern my masters the Pharisees, drive the Sadducees to plot my assassination, and alienate each friend I had in this room, Jew or Greek. I felt none of the fear they showed at the mention of Blastus the courtier. I was far more disturbed by the swelling of my most private member, and distracted by the presence of Esther, wife of Judah.

"I will see Blastus tomorrow when I go outside," I said. They would not be comforted by the surety with which I spoke, so I revealed one small part of my secret. "Blastus will do nothing to harm me. Like him, I am a Roman citizen."

Luke's bowl of spiced wine clattered to the floor. But his face held a wide, astonished grin. "You . . . ? When . . . ? You scoundrel!"

Ananias had remained silent through all of this. "Paul," he said to me now, "you must not mention to this man Blastus that you have become a follower of the Risen Christ."

Had I become a follower? I, a student of the Pharisees, a secret advisor to the despised court of Agrippa, a Jew citizen of the Roman empire, a Hebrew friend of a pagan Greek doctor? My identities were many, parts of me in conflict with other parts, so it was not hard to accept that I, the persecutor of the Jesus movement, had now become one of them as well. From Saul of Tarsus, I have inherited no clear distinction between True and False. I am all things to all men.

It is very late, and Judah frowns at me for the oil I am burning this long after the sun has set. Esther sleeps in the cordoned-off cubby, but I can envision her soft, lightly breathing form. I am disgusted with myself, because this plot in which I was embroiled . . . the persecution of the Jesus followers . . . was all part of Herod Agrippa's plans. Herod is King of the Jews by decree of Caligula Caesar, and my actions against the small, vocal Jewish sect were designed to ingratiate the king to the Pharisees. By killing! These Sarkate have too short an existence as it is, and there I was making it shorter still! I can see the face of the one called Stephen, the first follower of Jesus I had executed. They threw rocks at him, even though unsanctioned local execution is against Roman law. As he died he prayed. It must not have been the prayer related to medicine that Luke and Judah discussed earlier, for his God let him fall silent and die. And his death came at my direction, my command . . . sanctioned by Herod Agrippa, and passively allowed by the few Pharisees who knew it was taking place.

More disturbing still: I knew this Jesus of Nazareth. I despised how he twisted the words of the Law and the Prophets, how he declared that the

Kingdom of God was within man, not outside man. I worked secretly to incite the mobs who admired him, so that the blame for any violence his rabble committed against Rome might fall on him. But Jesus would have nothing to do with violence. He was not a great man, for great men inevitably wage war. Instead, he was just a decent man. And that made me hate him all the more.

One time, he looked right at me, during one of his many speeches. He had been talking about his followers as if they were sheep, and as if he were a shepherd guiding them. Then his eyes locked with mine. I was many, many paces back in the crowd, but I know he singled me out. Over the mob's head, to me, he said, "I have other sheep who do not belong to this flock. I must lead them, too. They will hear my voice."

I am blurring boundaries. I write as if I am indeed Saul of Tarsus. In the habit of being all things to all men, I cannot even be one thing to myself. I am nothing, to no one.

And I am inflicted by the fanciful imaginings of the Sarkate. For I cannot help but wonder whether Jesus was sending a message through Saul, to Paul, to me. I have searched the mind of Saul, and he has no idea what "other flock" Jesus meant.

The evil man called Saul of Tarsus is dead. He no longer lives; instead, I live through him. Tomorrow when I meet Blastus, I believe I shall greet him with the words, "How fare you, Blastus? I now follow the Risen Christ!" That should cause an interesting reaction. It will, at least, be a single step toward my becoming *something* to *someone* in this strange world of living matter.

Yours from among the Sarkate,
Paul of Tarsus

—10—

SENT BY: Lillian.Uberland@rsi.edu
RECEIVED BY: MNA@sellenville.edu

Kiss-Kiss, Cousin,

Brat! You should have given me more warning that you were going to change the format of Creationism Day! Twenty-four hours is *barely* enough time for me to redo what I've prepared. Were I lesser woman . . .

Ah, why go there? I'm not a lesser woman. But I am a woman who has a now-useless class lesson on her hands.

You're the public-school teaching expert, but I think you would have been proud of my methodology. I had an opening anticipatory activity, where I gave your kids the Answer, written on the chalkboard—just the number "12," pure and simple. Their task for the next two minutes: open their notebooks and write down the Question.

There'd be objections, naturally: "How are we supposed to know what the question was?!?" Once I convinced them to give it a try, though, I expected to get a nice variety. What's 6+6? How many doughnuts come in a box? What time does midnight happen? How many Apostles did Jesus have? (That last one would come from Mousy Girl or one of your other Fundies, of course.)

Then I would tell them: "You're wrong. All of you. The Question that goes with this Answer is, 'What number did Doctor Lillian Uberland just write on the chalkboard?'"

Remember what I said about "That's not fair!" being a Most Sacred Incantation among teenagers? How Dr. Hired Gun would use that to advance his "equal time for Creationism" education agenda? This was going to be my approach to cutting that down before it got a chance to grow. Because, as I would have told your kids, it really *isn't* fair to start throwing random Questions at the Answer. And, while it's fine to make guesses about what the right Questions might be, you can only get there by using what you know. The *only* thing they'd know about the number "12" on the chalkboard was that I'd put it there. And that, dear class, is lesson one in how real science is done.

The world we see today is one big Answer. What science does is struggle to find the right questions that lead to that answer. The best questions. Questions based on what we really *see* and *know.*

Contrasted with this is an approach that looks at the Answer, and already pretends to know what Questions led to it. Facts are just the filler, since the real Question is already assumed. And that's the approach of Creation "science," dear class. Today you'll be hearing a lot of ideas from Doctor Hired Gun, but whenever he's talking I'd like you to ask yourselves, "Does he really ask the right Questions? Is he really doing *science?*"

Because science, my little friends, does *not* pretend to understand everything, and *real* scientists spend most of their time trying to figure out what the right questions are. When they do think they're coming close to a good hypothesis, they immediately try to prove themselves wrong, testing to see if they've made a mistake somewhere. And if they don't work hard enough trying to prove themselves wrong, there are plenty of other scientists who'll be happy to do it for them.

This is what science gives the world: a whole collection of ideas that no one has been able to prove wrong yet.

Dr. Hired Gun here will agree that that's what science is. And then he'll claim that he can prove evolution wrong. But you know what? He'll say that proving evolution wrong is what makes his idea—that God created the Earth in exactly the way the Bible says—therefore right. It's a really safe claim for him to make. As a scientist, I can't pull out a spectrometer and measure God's wavelength. I can't spin God around in a centrifuge and tell you what God's made out of, layer by layer. And because I can't do that, Dr. Gun will claim that his ideas are just as scientific as mine. Because I can't prove him wrong.

That's another thing about science: it only deals with things you *can* prove wrong.

Let's go back to that number "12" I wrote on the chalkboard. I'm going to give you a different question, one you can't disprove. The question is: how many WinkiePoo spirits got together to create the universe? Answer: twelve. I'm sure you've heard of the WinkiePoos. They're powerful, noble creatures who soared through the empty universe without bodies, and one day, thousands of years ago, they decided to create the stars and the Earth by coughing up plasmic snot and shaping it into matter. They were especially careful with the Earth, giving it most of their creative energies. That's where man came from.

I'm telling you this story not just because it's fun to say "WinkiePoo." Whatever Dr. Hired Gun says while he's talking, he'll be starting with his own approved Question: "How does today's world show that in six days, God created the heavens and the Earth?" So it's only fair that you start with your own Question, too: "How does today's world show that the Twelve WinkiePoos created the heavens and the Earth from plasmic snot?" And whenever Dr. Hired Gun says something that *sounds* like it supports his Question, ask whether or not it also supports yours.

Do it right, and by the end of class today, you'll be faithful followers of the WinkiePoos. Or at least you'll know that asking the right questions is what science is all about.

What fun! What a lesson in the basics of scientific thinking!

But it's not to be. I don't get a classroom forum. I don't get a chalkboard to write on, and the students won't be at desks with their notebooks. Since you've moved us to the school auditorium, and since you'll have all your Biology classes in at once, I have to trash my whole approach. The method I planned requires a lot of personal interaction, one-on-one stuff to build rapport and trust, using the subtle play of looks and tones and laughs. But you've imprisoned me behind a podium, on a stage, in front of over a hundred kids. I'm reduced to a static lecture.

And do tell, Cousin, what's with inviting parents and the local media? Did you become a glory hound while I wasn't looking? Are you becoming more like *your* parents and *my* parents than I thought you were?

I have to make this short, since I now have a lecture to write. As well you know.

Your affectionate cousin,
Doctor Lillian

—11—

Greetings to my kind, the No-Flesh Asarkos,

There are times I am firmly entrenched in the memories of Saul. There are times I leave those memories, and concentrate only on my own thoughts. Stepping outside into the streets of Damascus was one of those latter times. I was caught up by a euphoria which you, my brethren Asarkos, may find either trite or incomprehensible.

Stars . . . in particular, this star, the sun of the Sarkate planet. We of our race know fully what suns are. They are highly compressed particles of matter, matter which would float free as gas if left to itself, but which, in stars, compress and fuse to create electromagnetic waves and other energies. The fanciful supposers among those of us who contemplate the sciences have suggested that stars are the one place that matter and energy live intermixed, one form converting with ease to the other. More practical thinkers of the Asarkos (which is to say, the vast majority of us) do not bother to think on such things. To us, stars are signposts that point to paths through the universe. They are useful when we keep ourselves far from them, allowing them to serve as beacons on our journeys through and between the galaxies. They are less useful when we draw too near to them, their mysterious power of attraction capable of shifting our wavelengths against our will, and sometimes distorting our paths through the continuum and our sense of passing time. Our supposers would see stars as metawave portals to new realities; to the rest of us, they are mere props on our cosmic stage.

Let me tell you, though you will not understand: there is no appreciating a sun until you see one through the eyes of the Sarkate. There is brilliance that hides all other stars. The sky above becomes a seamless whole, from horizon west to horizon east, a sweep that could be an entire universe unto itself. The eyes cannot bear to gaze upon a sun for too long; pain begins, and vision distorts in a way I like to think is analogous to our own Asarkos wavelengths being altered by the attractive force. I know that is not a literal comparison, but it should give our supposers more data to fancy over.

Seeing the sun and sky for myself helps me understand some of the oddities in the thoughts of Saul, why he believes the planet to be a single flat firmament, despite our friend Luke's insistence that the world is an orb, just as the moon and the sun are orbs. Saul's mind can acknowledge that information from Luke, but it does not understand how such a thing could be possible. So Saul's mind saw the world as a Sarkate serving platter—both circular, as Luke claimed, but also flat, as Saul's perception insisted. He thus accommodated both sets of data, and he remained confused about why he did not slip off the world, if his planetary serving dish were standing on edge as the sun and moon seemed to be.

In Saul's mind there are pillars supporting the plate, just as his Scriptures describe. The sky itself is not a coating of matter gases, but a large dome with lights embedded in it, blazing torches or even angels of the Lord keeping watch over the Earth. If only I had the power to give Saul the true data; he would be far more overwhelmed by the reality of the universe than by his people's guesses at what reality is like. That would elicit from him a truer, fuller praise of his God, and total comprehension of his Scripture, "The heavens declare the glory of God, and the Earth proclaims His handiwork."

Ah, the Earth—specifically, the city called Damascus, in the region called Syria. Here Saul would not gape in wonder, and it is I, the Asarkos named Paul, who must don the mantle of the neophyte. Judah and Luke escorted me into the outdoors of the planet. The streets of Damascus are lined with dwelling places three or four times the height of a man. The dwelling places are formed from non-sentient particle matter found on the planet's surface, re-crafted by man's cleverness into shells for their family groups. Simply put, man is a sentience inside a physical shell called flesh, which man further covers in clothing made from plants and animals, all of which dwells within a larger covering called a home or a shop or a tent or a palace. Man is layers upon layers, covering himself even to the point of creating the Law of the Jews. This the mind of Saul knows well. The Law of the Jews is an invisible covering, a fabric that sheaths the entire culture and holds it together as one people. But why? What Sarkate impulse underlies this layering, this hiding? For I have seen the sun with my own eyes today, and now I desire nothing more than to abandon the dwelling of Judah and feel this star's energy directly; to shed the clothing, so that every inch of my skin might absorb its warmth; and . . . now I speak against the mind of Saul, and outside my own references, giving voice to a feeling whose source I do not understand . . . to shed the Law and its confines, its shackles that keep me from running free and naked in this glorious, sunlighted world. The practical Asarkos, of which I am one, have it entirely wrong; using suns as signposts, we head away from them on pathways that carry us into the cold and dark of utmost space. We should move closer. We should be free.

All this talk of nakedness has given me stirrings for the wife of Judah. I must pause to compose myself.

—

I know that I pay too much homage to this single star, but please understand my reasons. I have been cut off from it for much of the day. My companions had to stuff me into a woven basket that is meant to carry grains.

I get ahead of myself in the story of the last two days' happenings, so allow me to speak of specific events, rather than obsessing on my feelings.

Shortly after dawn, Judah and Luke escorted me from our dwelling to a central meeting area several streets over from Strait Street, the lane on which we reside. There is a shallow but still active well in the area. It was the spot at which I was to meet Blastus, counselor to King Herod Agrippa, a counselor like me, as you might recall from my last epistle.

Blastus is no Jew, but a Roman born in Rome herself. He started life as a common man, trained to be a soldier, but was raised suddenly to authority on the passing whim of Caligula (long before that man became the Emperor Caesar). Caligula, walking one day outside of Caesarea with Herod Agrippa, had spotted Blastus drilling with his century in preparation for peacekeeping battles to be fought in the Germanic lands. Succumbing to his famed impetuousness, Caligula selected Blastus to be Agrippa's personal assistant and protector. As it would not do to allow Agrippa to be served by a commoner, Caligula granted Blastus the private ownership of an unremarkable plot of land owned by his uncle Tiberius, and a stipend that would be laughable to the truly wealthy *aristoi,* but staggering to a mere soldier. This exchange and promotion took place in a matter of moments, right on the preparation field. Blastus complied in stunned silence. Herod Agrippa accepted the appointee with cordiality and grace. Caligula, true to form, made a mocking irony of the event by demanding full-dress ritual formation and salute not only by Blastus's century, but by the five other centuries of his full cohort unit. Then Caligula marched the cohort in agmen columns, had them fall out into the acies fighting lines, and finally chided the six centurion commanders for appearing to be one soldier short of the minimum 480 fighting men.

To this day, Blastus wears his unearned nobility with gruff unease. Herod Agrippa likes him well enough, seeing in Blastus an earthier, more manly Roman than himself. It was Blastus who sponsored me for Roman citizenship. We are not friends. We are not enemies. He is blunt, unwavering in loyalty to Agrippa and to Rome, staid and uncomfortable at feasts within the House of Herod, immune to the flirtations of the court harlots. All this said, he is by no means a lout or ignoramus; quick to thought and slow to speech, it was he who first saw the wisdom in my plan of ingratiating Herod to both the Jewish Council and the Roman occupiers by focusing this land's unceasing unrest and frustration on a messianic band following a martyr named Jesus.

I give you much detail about this Blastus. I feel obliged to speak of him at length. Had it not been for him, I would not be writing these words right now. Rather, I would be dead at the hands of the Jews.

"You are late," Blastus said when I approached the well. Luke and Judah remained at the edge of the well yard, politely beyond an overhearing distance.

"Contemplations on the magnificence of the sunlight distracted me," I said. "The heavens declare the glory of God, and the Earth proclaims His handiwork.'"

Blastus looked to the sun. "It is hot," he said tonelessly. "This city reeks of dogs and sewage."

Smells are not a strong memory for Saul of Tarsus, so nothing about the scent of the city square seemed odd to me. I had no reply to Blastus's non sequitur. None, of course, save the non sequitur I would use to shatter Blastus's staid, stony facade.

"So, now," he said, "you are a follower of the Risen Christ."

Blastus knew without my telling him, no doubt thanks to rumors started by my dear, dear friend Luke. Luke is a wise man, brilliant even. Other Sarkate, both females and males, would deem him handsome in his darkened Greek way. He is quite humorous, as well. He simply lacks anything one might mistake for tact or restraint. I looked their way, to Judah and Luke, and Luke's head was already bowed in embarrassment. He knew that Blastus knew.

"That is correct," was all I could muster for response, disappointed as I was at being robbed of my moment of revelation.

"I am curious to know how this new twist fits with your plotting on behalf of our king and master." Blastus's tone, as ever, betrayed no real curiosity. He kept looking to the northern quadrant of the city, to his left, not meeting my eyes. He kept his arms crossed. They were very large arms, part of a very large body.

"Yeshua of Nazareth, whom we call Jesus, is the fulfillment of ancient Jew prophecies. He is the one long awaited by my people." Blastus still would not meet my eyes. It occurred to me that we had been speaking Latin, and that I had switched to the language as easily as when switching between Greek and Aramaic with Luke. "We call him the Anointed, Messiah, Christ, because he will take his place above all kings, and become the only king upon the face of the Earth."

"I know Jewish mythologies," Blastus said in a lackluster tone. "I myself have arrested any number of your long-awaited messiahs. I am eager for the part of your story that tells how this works to the betterment of Herod Agrippa."

I stopped what I was going to say next. The voice of Saul, from deep within me, screamed inside my mind, commanding, "No!" So I halted my retort, shocked at the strength of mind data I had not tried to access. I was going to say to Blastus, "Every knee shall bow and each tongue proclaim that Jesus the Christ is King, lord above Herod, lord above Caesar." Instead I simply let my mouth rest, dangling open. The prohibition against the words was nearly physical; Saul's flesh would not let Paul's mind give voice to those words. Not to this one, not to Blastus.

"No matter, then. There is plenty of time to explain. You can tell me your subtle reasonings through the door of your prison cell."

I shook myself from the paralysis of the flesh. "What do you say?" I demanded. "You're arresting me for my faith? This is no affair for the Romans!"

"I agree," Blastus said. "Your Jewish ideologies hardly interest me." There was rare emotion in his voice, and memory served to tell me that that was not a good sign. "I'm arresting you for unsettling the peace of the Roman province of Damascus."

"I have done nothing but sit in a house for ten days!"

Oddly, Judah and Luke had forsaken their positions and drawn near us. Odder still, Blastus drew a short sword I had not noticed, taken from a balteus about his shoulder that had been hidden by his long courtier's mantle. He did not hold it toward me or toward my companions. Instead, he faced the northern quadrant. I finally noticed the approaching Sarkate mob—each bearded like Judah, like me, a mob Jewish to the last man. They approached quietly, more than a score of them. Although I did not see any uniforms, I knew that three representatives of the Sanhedrin Guard would be among them. For had not I myself been the one to bring them here? Were they not my companions on the road to Damascus?

"I suspect this does not auger for our good." Luke's voice trembled . . . less, I think, from fear than from shame that it was his tongue that had rallied this mob.

"Dear friend, give in to no shame," I said. "You told them early what I would have told them today. We are safe in the power of the Risen Christ."

"Of course," Judah said. "Just as Stephen was safe from the mob you led."

Harsh words. Now the shame was mine.

The mob stopped when it reached the far side of the plaza. A single representative came forward, walking to the well to face us. I did not recognize the man. He was too young to be a leader of the synagogue, but old enough to be one of their students.

"Roman," he addressed Blastus, "we have come to detain and question Saul of Tarsus."

"I believe he is now called Paul," my well-informed fellow courtier said, "and I think you have really come to take his life." Blastus casually raised his sword, and the tip now aimed toward the man's most privileged member. "Paul of Tarsus is in my custody. Know that, and know too that I will not hesitate to improve upon your circumcision, Jew."

The man remained polite, although the hatred in his eyes belied his manners. "We would ask you to release him to us. We investigate a private Jewish matter of religion, and appeal to our sovereign right, granted by Rome herself, to try and punish our citizens in relation to such matters." He handed Blastus a parchment, and I recognized the broken seal of Caiaphus, High Priest of the Sanhedrin. It was the very letter of introduction I carried here from Jerusalem. I was to be the first victim of the hatred and threats I breathed.

Blastus barely glanced at the dispatch. "You are in Damascus. Our governor does not report to your priests."

"But we are in the Tetrarchy of Agrippa!" The man's patience faded quickly. The mob across the plaza edged forward. "Do you wish to risk the wrath of Herod, king by the grace of Gaius Caligula Caesar, by denying his people the courtesy of detaining one of their own, and one of Herod's own?"

Blastus smiled at him. It was not wise to elicit a smile from Blastus. "I am pleased you recognize him as one of Herod's own. For this very man, Paul of Tarsus, is a citizen of Rome, also by the grace of Caesar. No soldier stationed in Damascus would turn a blind eye to his illegal execution. Further, it is you who risks the king's anger. Do you not know that Paul of Tarsus is a counselor to the court of Lord Herod Agrippa?"

The mob's spokesman reddened. His lips pressed together tightly and his cheeks swelled.

To me, Luke whispered, "I shall never tire of being your friend. There is always something new to learn about you."

"Must you treat everything with flippancy?" Judah demanded of my Greek friend. "Is all the world just a quaint joke to you?"

Finally, the spokesman for the mob lost all pretense of control. "Blasphemer!" he screamed, pointing an accusatory finger at me. "A follower of false messiahs, and a traitor in service to the bastard, adulterous, false king! Death to Saul of Tarsus! Death to Herod Agrippa and to Rome!"

His shouts brought the synagogue's mob to life, and nearly resulted in the loss of his own. Blastus made good on his threat to improve the man's mark of faith; the Roman slashed a half dozen additional, small improvements on other parts of the man's flesh. We fled, leaving him wailing; a single sword cannot dissuade a mob, even a sword held by Blastus . . . in front of whom, I knew well, one should never say a negative word about King Herod Agrippa, tetrarch over Syria.

My Asarkos brethren, I leave you without a description of the confusion that followed; of our finding Esther, wife of Judah, and our being hidden in the homes of those who follow the Risen Christ; of the riots in the streets, a disturbance that had started as an issue of Jewish Law, but which drew in dissident Syrian and Persian residents, fires flamed by the tale of a Roman nobleman assaulting one of the occupied; of the governor's declaration that the Roman Blastus be found and charged with inciting two days of rioting; or of our final escape, each of us—Judah, Esther, Luke, Blastus, me—being lowered in baskets through a window on the city's outer wall, spirited away amidst a shipment of grain headed East toward Asia Minor.

I have no taste for describing what fear and violence are like. That is why I began this epistle with my praise of the Sarkate's sun. Think of that, my brethren, not of the Sarkate's violence. There is goodness in the sun. There is goodness in the Sarkate, and particularly among those who follow the Risen Christ. They hid us well and bravely, even me, their enemy.

We are far north now. I am glad to be able to leave the basket and once again, when it is day, to see the sun.

Yours from among the Sarkate,
Paul of Tarsus

—12—

SENT BY: Lillian.Uberland@rsi.edu
RECEIVED BY: MNA@sellenville.edu

Kiss-Kiss, Cousin,

Oh, no no no no you don't! I know exactly what you're up to. The only reason you wrote back to me on the very same night I emailed you was to distract me from writing my Creationism Day lecture. It won't work, sweetie . . . you won't suck me into the trap of gabbing the night away.

All right. Just one response to one comment, even though it puts me at risk of almost begging you to distract me from my purpose and benumbing my brain. *Just one!* I'll respond to the crack you made that "science and religion deal with different realities, so they're never really in conflict."

Hogwash, sweet cheeks. I know that's become a popular view, even among some scientists who don't want to think too hard about their role in life (or, more likely, who don't want to rock any boats that might sail on the sea of research funding). But there are only two options: a thing is real, or a thing is not real.

There is, I admit, that one very popular piece of propaganda that rears its head every decade, the claim that since science and religion examine "different aspects of experience," they never conflict with one another, per se. Science deals with physical things; religion deals with spiritual things. That mind fluff has gone by any number of names over the years; lately it's called NOMA, Non-Overlapping Magisteria, and it's batted about by scientists who feel they need to play nice with the religionists.

But think about it, Cousin. Even the use of the word "magisteria," a "realm of authority," is wrongheaded and arrogant. Scientists do not hold "authority" over reality; they just observe it, make inferences, and try to craft solid theories that withstand peer review. The moment a scientific idea becomes "true" because an "authority" says so, we've become no better than Creation scientists. There is no magisterium of science; theories survive our tests or they don't, in a manner not unlike natural selection.

I'm not just playing word games, either. Even assuming some "magisterium" for science, one would have to be blind to think religion didn't try to overlap with it, even rule over it. The most basic element of religion (in the West at least) is the "soul." This thing, this soul, is what we're all about, and the actions of our body will have a dramatic impact on its state. If I use my body for sin (and I do, as well you know, Cousin), then I am building up punishments for that soul when at last it parts from my body. If I turn that soul over to God for salvation, then the subsequent action of my body will determine what kind of rewards the soul gets in my afterlife.

Science deals with the body. Religion deals with the soul. But the soul relies on the body—my actions, my words, my behaviors, my excesses— for its eternal disposition, punishment or reward. Overlap much? I'd say so. There's some kind of exchange going on between my body and my spirit, but since religionists say the soul is "an immaterial substance," there's no way I can measure the exchange.

What the hell is an "immaterial substance"? You might as well say "a downward motion of great up-ness," or "I Am Who Am Not." If the soul is real, and my bodily actions have an impact on it, then there must be, in theory, some way of detecting the exchange. Something that doesn't violate the laws of conservation of energy.

Religionists would say I'm taking a sad, atheistic view to expect the soul to actually *be* something I might measure. Yet they have no problem telling me what measures my *body* has to take to ensure the salvation of my soul. They even want to legislate their ideas about souls into our classrooms, just to make sure we have a chance to get ourselves all moral and upright.

Fundies can't say what a "soul" is; nor, I might add, can they give it a *location*. It must be inside the body, but where? If I chop off a leg and survive, I don't think they'd say I've lost the leg-shaped part of my soul. So is my soul inside my head? Certainly chopping off my head would, they say, release my soul. So maybe my soul is inside my brain. But . . . what if I take drugs that alter my brain chemistry? Have I adjusted my soul? Are violent psychotics whose behavior is controlled by medication also getting the benefits of a soul upgrade . . . a mental metaphysic that cuts down on the punishments of their damned afterlives? Better after-living through chemicals?

So they can't say *what* a soul is; they can't say *where* it is. But they sure as heck can tell you *when* it is: the soul begins to exist from the moment of conception, and if you don't agree with that, they'll legislate their way right into your body. That sperm pops into that egg, and you, my friend, no longer have a say over its fate. That thing's got a human soul, and thou shalt not kill!

Hey . . . what if that fertilized egg accidentally breaks into a set of identical twins? That happens quite a bit. Does the soul also split? Do identical twins, who come from the same soul-imbued single cell, have to share a soul for their lifetimes? Is a second soul inserted later (meaning that one of the souls didn't exist at conception, as claimed)? Better still, what about heterozygous births . . . a single individual who grew from two separately fertilized eggs that joined. Not as common as identical twins, but it still happens. Does that person have *two* souls? Can one soul go to heaven, the other to hell?

Enough, enough, enough . . . I'm getting tiresome even to myself. I just wanted to make my point. "Non-Overlapping Magisteria," the idea that science and religion deal with different "realities," is a crock. Scientists who prattle on about it are hucksters for the wrong side. Religion will always, in practice, try to inject its spiritual beliefs into the realm of the physical.

None of this is anything I can say tomorrow. Now I'll be up even later, thank you very much. Perhaps if I pray to my Twelve Great WinkiePoo spirits, I'll find the strength to create yet another fantastic presentation.

But believe me, my conniving, distracting little Cousin . . . your Christmas present is going to *suck* this year.

Your affectionate cousin,
Doctor Lillian

−13−

Greetings to my kind, the No-Flesh Asarkos,

Roman, Greek, Jew, Asarkos . . . Blastus, Luke, Judah, me. What am I doing on this planet? Why have I abandoned my search for our Ten Who Are Missing? Why have I allowed sentient matter creatures, a curiosity, to become an obsession?

We travel north toward Asia Minor now, a party of despair. Often tempers are short, and for the smallest of reasons we become angry with one another. Yesterday I saw a goat and misidentified it as a dog. Judah corrected me brusquely. I tried to speak more of it, saying that goats and dogs seemed very similar to my eyes, and that one of the breeds must have developed from the other, since they strike me as less dissimilar in flesh than hulking, pale Blastus is from darkened, wiry Luke.

The suggestion infuriated Judah. "They are not breeds, they are separate kinds! The Scriptures say that the Lord created each animal to mate according to its kind, and to suggest that goats grew from dogs or dogs from goats is to speak against the Scriptures of the Lord!"

It is easy to forgive Judah; Esther has been ill, and her infirmity has slowed our progress. Judah pretends to be angry with her weakness, but I know he is frightened for her. Luke looks after her, but curses the desert and its lack of healing herbs. He seems to be taking the absence of medicines personally.

It is easy, as well, to forgive Luke's sullenness. He has not said a word about his inadvertent reporting of my baptism in the manner of the followers of Christ. He pretends to accept my consolation, my assurance that I was going to cause the same commotion he had caused. But I am not fooled. Luke is not consoled. Luke is bitterly furious with himself.

And Blastus, my dear fellow counselor. Our nobleman-soldier, sword-bearing protector, committed citizen whose very loyalty to Agrippa and Rome has made him an outlaw, the man named as the cause of the outbreaks in Damascus. "I will appeal to Caesar," he said our first day out of the grain baskets, a half-day north of the nearer oases and already well into the deserts. "It is the right of every Roman citizen to appeal his case to Caesar. No governor's edict can supercede the Emperor's word." Blastus travels with us, but looks at none of us. He especially does not look at me. He takes no action against us, and he hazards no display of feeling, but I can sense that behind his stoic facade, there roils a sea in tempest. His agitation is greatest at sunset, when we make camp; it has been years since he journeyed a wilderness with his old cohort, but I suspect he is frustrated that we dig no protective entrenchment about our camp, as is the nightly practice of a Roman troop. But that is just one of many frustrations Blastus hides.

A natural habit for an Asarkos: I tried to extend an interchange tendril to retrieve information on Blastus's thoughts.

You, my brother Asarkos, see nothing odd in my attempt to do that. But I am a creature of flesh now, and there is no reaching out beyond what the flesh contains. So strange, it seems to me right now, to find the fullness of my being engulfed, compressed, contained within this negligible speck of flesh. Everything is so small, here in the higher wavelengths. And though it seems to me that passing time proceeds apace as ever, I have estimated the turnings of the planet . . . I live at an unthinkable pace, faster than the fastest thoughts of the greatest thinkers of the Asarkos. The Earth turns once and a day is gone; a Sarkate is granted scarce more than twenty thousand of those turns, and his life ends. Yet to us . . . we the bodiless, we the Asarkos . . . twenty thousand rotations are a mere handful of oscillations, barely enough time to think deeply about what we are seeing. I say to you, "Man is born, man grows, man grows old, man dies." And in the time it takes you to receive and share those data among all members of our race, it has already happened to a generation of men here among the Sarkate.

It is relativity of perception. They are a flicker of starlight to us; we would be slow, plodding aeons to them. Had I hesitated in my flight from Our Enemies, evaded them for a time in their own wavelengths and made my dash to higher realms a dozen moments later, I would not even be here among these particular Sarkate—Luke my sullen friend, Judah my bitter host, Blastus my tormented colleague, and lovely, lovely Esther, now so ill. A little hesitation on my part, and they would have been long dead. I would have arrived a hundred years in their future; in our future. And what would I have seen here? Would Blastus's glorious Rome dominate the entire sphere? Would Luke's sciences have won out over his deities? Would the Jews have hunted down and killed the followers of Christ? Or would the followers of Christ have swelled in number, themselves a force to be contended with?

Would Caesar have what Caesar wants? Would God still reign as God?

"Damn the heat," I heard Blastus say, his first words in many days. "Damn the desert."

I responded carefully. "It will be cooler soon. The day is ending." We were on our own now. The Jew followers of Christ who smuggled us to safety had parted ways with us earlier that day, heading east to barter grain in Mesopotamia. Our party was to continue due north into Asia Minor, to the city of Antioch where Judah has kinsmen.

"It will get too cold," Blastus said. "Damn the cold."

"I shall line your blanket with the spare ewe's hide. Sleep inside tonight. You've spent every night under the stars, and the air is always biting."

"Tents," Blastus said. "Damn tents."

I surprised myself on this journey. I discovered I was an accomplished maker of tents, both at shaping and sewing the fabrics, and at fashioning supports. I can twist and cure ropes as well. Our first night out in the open, while fear still peaked the pace of my heart, my hands fell naturally to the task of preparing our site for the evening's sleep. It seems I find more of the knowledge and skills of Saul of Tarsus when I am tired or distracted or distraught; they rise to the surface and fill the gap left by my mental inactivity. I'd halfway prepared the folds and fastenings of my first tent before realizing what I was doing; the others showed no surprise at my speed and deftness, and then I was able to remember so many, many times I had done the same sort of preparations. It was my main craft for supporting myself, back before I was an Asarkos sentient inside a Sarkate form.

"Do not disparage tents, Blastus," I said kindly. "They are like another body to us. They are small temples to protect us from the harshness of the world."

"Don't play rabbi to me." He crossed his arms angrily. He does that often.

"I said nothing religious."

"You were about to."

There were no more words beyond those. But Blastus sleeps inside his tent this night.

I tire, my brother Asarkos, and I too must sleep. It is strange, but I worry for Blastus, who among those of this party is least like a friend to me. He feels great things within himself, yet is too disciplined to let them show. And I fear that the less he acts on those feelings, the less, in the long run, he will truly be able to feel.

⤙

Sleep is a period of time involving the temporary cessation of sentience. The Sarkate, being complex material constructs with diverse energy intake needs, voluntarily submit to the state of sleep. I suppose it is voluntary, but I know that should a Sarkate neglect sleep for an extended period, perhaps four or five rotations of the planet, then the flesh itself would command a period of unconsciousness. I do not understand how matter can contain mind. Even less do I understand how particulate substance can dominate over the will of a immaterial sentient.

I do know this, that sentience does not cease entirely during the periods called sleep. A "dreaming" state can ensue, as if mind were restless with the darkening forced upon it by matter.

This, the following, I dreamed last night quite clearly. It was a dream constructed entirely of words, with no images. That means I must have dreamed it with the part of my mind not accustomed to visual sight. I dreamed it with my Asarkos mind. And the part of my mind that is Sarkate dreamed back at me, using the words of Saul.

Saul said, *At first I thought you were an angel. Then I thought perhaps a demon.*

I said in Aramaic, Who are you, sir?

Saul said, *Now, the Pharisees, they believe in angels and in demons. The Sadducees do not; theirs is a far starker universe, with a far more distant God.*

I said in Greek, Who are you, lord?

He said, *I am Saul, whom you possess.*

And I said, I am Paul, of Tarsus.

He said, *I know you, Paul. You are the creature with no body. You come from where the stars are.*

I said, I am sorry I killed you.

Saul said, *Perhaps it is for the best.* He sounded very sad. He did not seem pleased to be Saul of Tarsus.

I said, Your race is fascinating. You are very fascinating. I have been reading the memories you left behind.

Saul said, *I have been reading your mind as well. You do not like me at all.*

I said, True, I do not.

Saul said, *And I see that you lust for the body of Esther, wife of Judah.*

I said nothing. I felt great shame.

Saul said, *Do not disparage yourself. The flesh was a great burden for me. It is my sin you struggle with, not your own.*

I still said nothing.

Saul said, *You have written to your people about the glories of the flesh. You mentioned in earlier epistles that you felt lust for Esther. Then you stopped writing of that, and I could tell that you were struggling with shame. As Adam covered his nakedness from the Lord, so you hide your feelings from your brethren, omitting the words that might reveal your greatest shame.*

I said, I know. I know, but what should I do?

Repent, Saul said, *and believe upon the name of the Lord Jesus Christ, that you might be saved.*

I said, This is your advice to me? You, who persecuted the followers?

Saul said, *I have seen the world through your eyes, heard it through your ears, felt it anew with your bowels. There is more to the universe than the Law, the Prophets, and the petty intrigues of Herod's court. I see now that I was railing against the will of heaven itself.*

I said, This is a strange dream. How could the hater of an idea so quickly become that idea's proponent?

Saul said, *You have much to learn about the ones you call the Sarkate. Of how flesh exists in uneasy truce with its own appetites, always at risk of self-enmity, even outbreaks of rebellion against the mind it carries.*

I said, The flesh is yours, the mind is mine, and I do not wish to be your enemy.

Saul said, *Yes. This is my body. Please know that I am not your enemy. Know that, Paul of Tarsus.*

I said, I have already told you that. Let us stop debating it. It is ridiculous to be arguing with a dream.

Saul said, *Dreams are random. Dreams are scattered and nebulous. This is too coherent to be a dream.*

When I understood what he meant, I demanded, Are you not a dream? Am I wrong, and is Saul of Tarsus still alive?

But by then he had stopped talking, and I stopped dreaming, and I slept for many more hours. We arose at daybreak, we the party of despair. We ate, we sat silently, we do not speak. Today is Sabbath, and Judah insists we must not travel on this day. But tomorrow we again head north.

Yours from among the Sarkate,
Paul of Tarsus

−14−

SENT BY: Lillian.Uberland@rsi.edu

RECEIVED BY: MNA@sellenville.edu

Kiss-Kiss, Cousin,

Gross understatement time: "Well, Cuz, that didn't go as expected."

How's your head? The doctor said you'd be fine, but "fine" to an M.D. doesn't necessarily mean a lot in terms of actual pain. It's just a survival assessment.

In fairness to your Fundamentalist students and their parents, I don't think their church should have to pay for damages to the school property. That crowd of protesters . . . about two hundred of them, if you can trust the newscasts . . . were obviously out-of-towners. At first, when I drove up, I was amused. "They're protesting the free exchange of ideas in science classrooms?"

But I got nervous when I saw the signs. Did you catch any of them? I mean before you were knocked unconscious, of course. One woman had a sign that said, "EVIL-utionists will burn in HELL." No surprise to that sentiment, but the sign's lettering was done in lavender. Lavender! I had visions of being stoned to death by powder puffs. Another sign, held by a tattooed guy who looked more like a biker than a Sunday school fanatic, said, "Seven Days, Seven Nights. Not just a good idea, it's the

Law." I presume he meant the law of God, since that one's not on the U.S. books yet.

The one who started it all (not the one who knocked you out; that one didn't get away like most of the others, and the cops have him dead to rights since the news cameras were rolling right on you during the assault) was a balding, middle-aged fellow in a blue turtleneck. If I'd seen him in any other context, I'd figure him for being as nice as nice can be. Somebody's quiet, patient Dad, hanging around the schoolyard, unobtrusively waiting for Johnny or Jeannie to get out of band practice. No derogatory sign in this guy's hands. No yelling or chanting, and he didn't even join in the group-hymn sing-alongs. He just stood there nodding pleasantly at the others, looking casually around the crowd, until he spotted me.

That man beelined straight through the mob and intercepted me on my way to the front doors. I wasn't going to stop, Cuz, honest. Wasn't going to say a word to any of them. But he'd obviously been waiting for me, me specifically. He stopped dead in front of me, planted his feet, crossed his arms, and said with a snarl, "Madame, I will be *praying* for you."

Me and my mouth. I could have said "Okay," and stepped around him, but instead I decided to have one of my Mark Twain wisecrack comeback moments. "Gee thanks!" I said, "'cause I'm awful busy doing all the *thinking* for the likes of *you*."

He smacked me, open palm, I fell to one knee, he screamed curses in the name of Jesus, he shoved me down the rest of the way, I cried like a weak little idiot, blah blah blah, I'm sure you read the rest of it in the papers. I balled myself up on the ground. I expected him to kick me, Michael. He was out of his mind, so I covered my face to wait for the worst. That's why I didn't see the fighting start.

Who was fighting? What other group was there? The police asked me that over and over, but I couldn't tell them. All I saw in front of the school were protesting Christian Fundamentalists. When I risked looking up, people were punching each other, and metal trash cans were being thrown through the school windows, from the outside in. I remember thinking, "What if there are kids on the other side of those windows?" I remember thinking, "Hey, there are kids out *here*, running among the rioters!"

That's when I saw you, shoving through the crowd toward me. As shocked as I was from the attack, and as embarrassed as I was for cowing under it like . . . like, a *girl* . . . I was caught up by the craziness for a moment. Your eyes were on fire. Someone must have told you they'd attacked me, because you were scanning the grounds, frantic, completely oblivious to any danger to yourself. A rock just missed you, a big one. Did you know that? You were so focused on finding me, you didn't even seem to notice. When you spotted me, you walked right up to four rioters who were pounding on a fifth man, you *shoved* them aside with both hands, your eyes still fixed on me, and your hair blew back, tousled and mussed in the way I think is so sexy. Something was burning, the first of three small fires, and way behind you the rising smoke swirled as your backdrop, scattering the sunlight and blocking backlight so you darkened. It was like the cover of a tacky romance novel. I even caught my breath—my hero, crashing through the mob, heedless to his own safety.

Then, of course, that guy hit you on the back of the head with his sign and you dropped like a sack of cement.

I'll tell you, Mikey, you must be one hell of a beloved teacher. Three of your strapping, young schoolboys were immediately over you, calling your name and trying to revive you. When it was obvious you wouldn't be rising from the dead any time soon, they stood up, shoulder to shoulder in a triangle surrounding you, backs in, faces glaring outward at the mob. The four rioters you'd crashed through finished up their pummeling of the poor unfortunate they'd selected, and they started toward you and your schoolboys. They were ugly fellows, walking evidence that parts of the universe couldn't possibly have sprung up from Intelligent Design. They looked like they'd chew those kids up, and swallow you for dessert.

The kid closest to them, a lanky, befreckled redhead whose name I never found out, held up a hand and yelled at the thugs, "Stop, in the name of the Lord!" My head heard it wrong at first. I thought he'd said "name of the law," but a second later I concluded he really had said Lord. It dawned on me. Those three kids were *them*. They were from your group of seven Fundies who'd started all this trouble.

And damn it, Mikey, the thugs stopped right in their tracks. Three of them even looked scared, who knows why. The fourth thug (the lowest among equals in that lovable brain trust of hairless bipeds) shook the startle off his face and kept going toward the boy. Eyes slit; face unshaved; teeth gritted; fists clenched.

Then, *boom, boom* . . . ass flattened. Mikey, your redhead Fundie kid popped him twice, fast, and knocked the wind out of him! I doubt Wonder Thug even knew what happened; by the time he woke up he was already in police cuffs, staggering and dazed while they led him away, his brains still lost in an impenetrable fog brought on by your fightin' freckled Fundie.

They wouldn't let me get in the ambulance with you. They wouldn't let me follow in my car, either, because they wanted the EMTs to check me out right there on the scene. There was absolutely nothing wrong with me . . . and that made me even more embarrassed, since I'd been such a baby about it. The news people wanted to talk to me, but your Fundie kids wouldn't let them. The Fundie kids wanted to talk to me but the police wouldn't let *them*. The police wanted to drill me, and all I could think about was whether or not you would live. That sounds overly dramatic now that I know it was just a concussion, but I was terrified, Cousin. I needed to get to you and hold you, make the insanity go away, cradle you tenderly the way I did back in the crazier days, when all we had for escape from our overdriven, hyper-achieving families were each other's arms and embrace.

Now that you're fine, don't expect any more sentimentality like that any time soon. And don't you *ever* get yourself knocked out again. Hear me?

A side note to all this: at the hospital, I think I met your Mousy Girl student. I can't be sure, since you just don't walk up to people and say, "Hey, are you a kid I don't know who I call Mousy Girl behind her back?" But she fit your description to a tee, stringy brown hair, eyes downcast, and a sad little smile. Cute as a bug's ear, in her passive way. I saw her when I left your room, a few hours before you were discharged. Her mother was asking for you by name, so I figured it had to be someone who knew you from school. And my gut was on full Fundie alert, which made me realize it might be Mousy.

When they walked my way, I said hello to them and told them I was your cousin. Woo-boy . . . did that mother ever size me up, scalp to shoes in a deliberate evaluation. She didn't look at all pleasant about it, either. Attila the Mom. "So," she said, "are you happy about what you and your science have caused?"

Normally I'd be furious and lash out (yeah, yeah, believe it or not). But as the mother brushed past me, daughter following behind, Mousy stopped long enough to touch my hand. "It's all right," she whispered, never raising those sad eyes. And I realized it was, just because she said so.

You start back up at school tomorrow. Here's hoping the rest of your semester is a little less eventful. Me, I'm headed back to my fruit flies. They're a raging mob, too, but they're not quite so opinionated. Or dangerous.

Your affectionate cousin,
Doctor Lillian

—15—

Greetings to my kind, the No-Flesh Asarkos,

It is two days since I wrote my last epistle. The wife of Judah is still too sick for us to move north. We are only three days' walking from the out-skirts of Antioch, but it appears we can go no further, at least not until Esther is well. Our fear of pursuit from Damascus has kept us far east of the primary road; now we regret that decision, as we would likely have made our destination late last week had we kept to the main way. At the very least, we could have beseeched the aid of other travelers.

This morning our party discussed the option of sending a messenger forward to bring help and faster transportation from Antioch, but it could not be settled who should go. Certainly not Judah; he is frightened to leave Esther's side, and was nervous about being away from her even for the short duration we grouped together, outside her tent, to weigh our options. Nor would Luke run ahead; he is the other physician among us, and I suspect he fears Esther may die while he is off finding aid. Sullen as he is these days, that would very well push him beyond mental limits he could tolerate. He would blame himself, and expect Judah to blame him as well. So Luke will continue testing Esther's extremities for heat or cold, continue mixing his barley ptisans of black hellebore and anise, continue trying to get the comatose Esther to take some of the concoction between her lips.

As for Blastus and me, there was not even discussion of one of us going. Neither courtier of Herod Agrippa is now trusted by Judah, husband of Esther. My only contribution is to help keep her comfortable in her hour of suffering.

For reflecting both the light and the heat of the sun, no color fabric is better than white, provided the fabric is thick enough or backed with hide to eliminate translucence. Disassembling the blanket I had made for Blastus, I constructed a shading barrier for Esther's tent. Using lashed branches from the wasteland's dead, wild olive trees, I was able to construct two poles rising high above our heads. I affixed shorter branches at raised angles from the tops of the first two poles. Between the angled extensions, I strung the sheep-hide blanket. At the right distance east of Esther's tent, the blanket could be raised to throw a shadow over most of the sunside. Luke assisted me in setting a stone foundation for the two poles, that they might stand without human support. We lashed cross branches between the length of the two principal poles so that any wind, unlikely as that would be today, would not dislodge the makeshift shader.

"She has passed no bile today," Luke said, "neither the yellow nor the black. I need stronger purgatives."

I moved two of the heavier stones he had just laid upon the base. "Not so solid for the foundation," I told him. "As the day progresses, we will need to reposition the poles."

"Of course, yes." Luke seemed ashamed that he had not been the one to realize it. "As the sun traverses the sky, the shade will shift."

"I wish I had more material," I complained. With sufficient stock, I have in the past constructed tents within tents, using a layering strategy to block the harshest of the sun's rays, combined with a positioning and airing strategy that maximized the flow of light wind. I can eliminate the stifling stillness of a closed tent even without the preferred Cilicium tenting cloth. "It is not that the sun traverses the sky," I said casually to my physician friend. "It is the spinning of the planetary orb that creates that illusion. The sun, from our perspective, is fixed in the cosmos. Our spinning world grants us the illusion of its movement."

Luke gave me a queer look. In strange tones, he said, "That could very well be, I think. Do you really believe the sun is fixed in the heavens?"

"No, of course not." I stood up from the stone-pile foundations, satisfied that the configuration was now firm enough to hold the poles, yet loose enough for us to move easily and quickly later. "The sun, too, moves through the heavens. But we are held in its attractive force, so from our perspective, and from the perspective of the rest of the debris it holds in orbits, it remains fixed while we spin and circle it."

"What other debris do you mean?" Luke seemed to be having trouble selecting the words he wanted to use to question me.

"Some of the other lights in the sky at night. Other orbs that seem to be stars, but which are not." I tested the nearer principal pole with a finger. Solid. I was pleased.

"Ah. Planets. Tell me what you think of the 'Epic of Kirta,'" Luke asked.

It was an odd question, one that related to nothing we had been discussing. "I have no opinion," I said. "I have wanted to read the text, but have only seen your scribed copy, written in Ugaritic, a tongue barbaric to my understanding."

"And yet," said Luke, "a tongue you are speaking with me right now."

I laughed, then stopped. Ugaritic is an ancient language of the Phoenicians. Since I had been speaking of stars in the heavens . . . the Phoenicians were a seafaring race, much attuned to the movements of the heavens . . . speaking in that tongue had seemed natural.

Yet Saul of Tarsus did not know that language. It had been ages since anyone spoke the tongue; these days it was only read, not spoken. Luke could read Ugaritic texts.

"At first your vowel sounds confused me," Luke said, switching to Greek. "They were different from my expectations, closer to Hebrew than to Aramaic. But it makes sense."

Perhaps to him. I was not certain what he meant.

Luke picked up one of the dried olive branches we had rejected in our construction of the sheep-hide shader, and began etching characters in the dried dirt. As he etched, I read aloud the Ugaritic poetry he scribed:

> You must give me Lady Huraya,
> The Fair One, your firstborn child!
> Who is as fair as the goddess Anath, Who is as comely as
> Astarte;
> Whom God gave me in my dream,
> The Father of Man in my vision.

"Well translated," Luke said, forlorn. I did not think it possible, but his demeanor showed more dejection than before.

"The language is not altogether dissimilar from Hebrew," I suggested.

"In much the way Greek is not altogether dissimilar from Latin, I suppose," Luke said. "No. This language you do not know. It is impossible for you to know it. Impossible."

I should note we had not set eyes on my colleague Blastus for some time. That comes to mind now because at this point in my story, Judah came running from the tent, very frantic.

"Her breathing turns phlegmatic!" he cried, and then struggled to catch his breath. "We must get her to where there are softer beds and better medicines! Pack camp, and send Blastus toward Antioch for help. Send the unbelieving pagan, I will accept even his help now!"

It did not take more than a quick glance around our camp to determine that Blastus was nowhere to be found.

"Curse him! Damnation upon him for abandoning us!" Judah hollered. Then he wailed, a sound more like an animal than like a Sarkate. I thought back, back to Judah's furious insistence that goats and dogs could in no wise be related to one another, that each bred true according to its own kind. I felt shame. In his hour of torment, I should not have let thoughts of animals enter my head. I should not have pondered even for a moment, when I heard his inhuman wail, how similar the Sarkate are to the other matter creatures wandering the face of this orb.

"He has not abandoned us," Luke said quietly. He sat upon the dry earth, using the olive branch to erase the Ugaritic words. "He left shortly after our morning discussion, angling northwest toward the main road to Antioch. He runs with the speed of a gazelle, even in the heat of day. He is a nobleman, but he is always a soldier. He has physical endurance we cannot comprehend. I would not be surprised if he were almost at the gates of the city by now."

Judah's face showed the faintest glimmer of hope. His taut cheeks and curled lips relaxed.

"Nothing, these days, would surprise me," Luke said.

—

I write again, much later on this same day. Far in the distance, we see the rising of the dried wasteland dust. The sun wanes, day ends. The rising dirt is Blastus, no doubt. The speed of his approach can only mean that he arrives in a chariot, a Roman chariot, commandeered from the legion stationed at Antioch. Blastus is fast; he has outpaced to Antioch the news of his own outlaw status.

To no avail, however. For moments ago, Esther, the wife of Judah, died. Blastus will curse himself for missing a victory by mere minutes. I will console him, telling him that she, in any case, would not have survived the harsh chariot ride back to the city. But my words will be ineffectual; Blastus, I am sure, has put much faith in the success of this rescue that Esther did not live to see.

Judah has torn his outer garments in lamentation. Luke sits expressionless, still in the dirt. I have tears running from my Sarkate eyes, rolling down and catching themselves in my wetted Sarkate beard.

I did not simply lust after Esther, wife of Judah. I grew to love her. Now she is gone, she whom I loved, gone in the twinkling of an eye.

Yours from among the Sarkate,

Paul of Tarsus

—16—

INTERNET RELAY CHAT

IRC CHAT LOG: from IP Address 38.22.85.199

Host Name 5YRc1.sellen-edu - Private Room mode

Begin text capture

    from **MICHAEL**91773: Lily, are you there?

    from **MICHAEL**91773: Is this thing working?

    from **MICHAEL**91773: I'm just talking to myself, aren't I?

    from **DR-LILY**: Kiss kiss, Cousin!

    MICHAEL91773: Finally. You're as on-time as ever, Lillian. I wasn't even sure this thing was working.

    DR-LILY: How is my Mikey? Has his head healed up all better?

    MICHAEL91773: It's just fine, thank you. I can't believe you've got me using this thing to have conversations. Mind telling me how this is better than a phone call?

    DR-LILY: It's the future, Mikey. One day, the whole world will be talking like this without long-distance charges!

    MICHAEL91773: I live twenty minutes from you, in the same area code.

    DR-LILY: Details, details. Frightens me to think that the minds of the next generation are in the care of technophobes like you.

    MICHAEL91773: I'm not a technophobe! I just don't understand what benefit talking through email has over talking by phone.

DR-LILY: A "chatroom talk," or an "online chat." You have to learn the vocabulary words, Mikey.

MICHAEL91773: Whatever. How's work?

DR-LILY: Stimulating. Frustrating. My next generation of *Drosophila* have graduated from pupae school, but I can't duplicate any of the eye-scaling traits of that doomed batch of flies. I still can't even determine whether the mutation was natural or artificially induced.

MICHAEL91773: Well, if you weren't doing anything to induce it, it had to be natural, right?

DR-LILY: Nyet, nyet, Cousin. I could have screwed something up. It might not be genetic . . . maybe I allowed contaminants in, or made mis-steps. Could be anything or everything. "Science means always having to say you're sorry."

MICHAEL91773: Is that a reference I'm supposed to catch? Where's it from?

DR-LILY: Sigh, never mind. For only being four years younger than me, you are *such* a kid. So, here's what I face. If the variation is genetic, where does it occur? I've only got four fruit-fly chromosomes to select from, but even there I don't know where to start. I've studied nearly every form of naturally occurring variation—short winged, curly winged, yellow skins, ebony skins, white eyes, eyeless, you name it. I've started down the path of variations on the eyeless mutation, located on chromosome 2. But what if these huge, scaly growths are related to antennopedia? I'm on the wrong chromosome altogether!

MICHAEL91773: Lily Lily Lily Lily!! You're boring me to tears.

DR-LILY: Whoops. I forgot that you became a public school teacher because you didn't want to think too hard about the basics of biology.

MICHAEL91773: Why do you always have to pick on me like that?

DR-LILY: Because I love you and want to make you strong. I'm the force of natural selection in your life.

MICHAEL91773: That wouldn't benefit me, just my offspring.

DR-LILY: Whoa, a real live evolution joke from Mikey! Well, if it's offspring you want, a little selective breeding may be in order (wink, wink . . .).

MICHAEL91773: That reminds me. I wanted to ask a question about animal breeding. Isn't a lot of Darwin's natural selection theory based on observation of the breeding of farm animals?

DR-LILY: (I flirt, he talks about farm-animal sex. I'm getting worried.) Answer: yes, that influenced Darwin, probably even more than his observations in the Galapagos. Why do you ask?

MICHAEL91773: Well, isn't it kind of a jump to go from human selection like forced breeding, to a theory about natural selection as the main force of evolution? Breeding isn't natural selection.

DR-LILY: Says who?

MICHAEL91773: Says common sense! It's Human Selection, human beings artificially deciding what traits are good and what traits aren't. Whether it's cows, dogs, cats, whatever.

DR-LILY: And when did you decide that humans aren't part of nature? When a pack of cheetahs weed out the sick and young antelope at dinner time, would you call that unnatural Cheetahal Selection?

MICHAEL91773: Hmm. Okay, but look. We breed cows to have more meat on them. It helps the people who eat the cows. And let's face it, being meatier is the very thing that *lowers* the cow's chance at survival. It's more likely to end up on a dinner plate.

DR-LILY: Mikey love, you're missing the most basic thing about natural selection. It isn't about survival of the individual; it's about survival of the species. More basic still, it's about the survival and adaptation of the genes. Before they get fed to the humans, meatier cows get to have meatier cow babies. Skinny cows don't get to breed, and the gene line is cut off. So if cow genes know what's good for them, they'll keep their cows nice and plump, thus allowing lots of kiddy cows to be born.

MICHAEL91773: All right, here's another one. When humans stop interfering with breeding, doesn't an animal herd just revert back to its normal traits? Don't all the forced variations disappear?

DR-LILY: Natch. You see that in fruit flies, too. Takes about nine or ten generations, unless, of course, you happen to be *my* mutant fruit flies, who impolitely die before passing on their scaly eyes to the next generation . . . grumble, grumble.

MICHAEL91773: So if all the changes aren't permanent, doesn't that mean selection, natural or not, isn't permanent?

DR-LILY: Mikey, evolution works over millions of years, not over dozens of generations. Fatter cows will slip toward the average weight, given a few more generations of breeding. But give them two million years of recurring famines and drought, and *only* the fatter lineage of cow will survive.

MICHAEL91773: Great. Now, is it true that scientists have never created a new species that could breed?

DR-LILY: That's true. But heck, even within a species, mating can get tricky. You would *not* want to see a female Chihuahua give birth to a St. Bernard's puppies.

MICHAEL91773: That's a good one, thanks!

DR-LILY: Cousin, why do I get the feeling you're taking notes?

MICHAEL91773: 'Cause I am. These are all questions a friend asked me, and I didn't know how to answer all of them.

DR-LILY: So you have me teaching a science class by proxy?

MICHAEL91773: Lillian, you're arrogant and sarcastic, but you're the smartest person I know. When my friend hears your answers, they'll probably give me more questions. Mind if I run the ones I don't know by you?

DR-LILY: I'd be pleased to help. And may I point out that your singular friend mysteriously became plural when you needed to refer to "them" with a pronoun? This leads me to believe that maybe our friend has boobs. Are we dating, Mikey?

MICHAEL91773: No! Are you serious? Definitely not!

DR-LILY: I'll take that to mean "yes," then.

MICHAEL91773: Just one more question, Lily. Do you know what "speaking in tongues" is? Also called "glossolalia," I think?

MICHAEL91773: I guess you don't know anything about it, huh?

MICHAEL91773: Lily? Hello?

MICHAEL91773: Are you still there?

DR-LILY: I'm here.

MICHAEL91773: Well?

DR-LILY: My turn to ask a few things. Seeing your questions about evolution bounce easily into questions about speaking in tongues makes me wonder . . . is our new "friend" a member of a Fundamentalist church?

MICHAEL91773: Well, yeah.

DR-LILY: The very church that incited a mob to knock you to the ground unconscious?

MICHAEL91773: That's not fair, Lily. You said they shouldn't be held responsible for that mess. The DA is only filing charges against the one who assaulted me, and that guy isn't even from their church.

DR-LILY: It was a "yes" or "no" question, Michael.

MICHAEL91773: Yes. It's Giselle, Lindsey's mother. "Mousy Girl," I mean, that's what you call Lindsey.

DR-LILY: Giselle. Nice name, *tres chic*. And all these questions spring from your desire to have swell conversations over coffee with her?

MICHAEL91773: No. All right, all right. They asked me to speak at their church. They're gonna let me give a talk on evolution, no debate even. So I went this past weekend. With Giselle and Lindsey, kind of a pre-visit to get the lay of the land. During the service, there was a lot of praying out loud in different languages, so that's why I was wondering if you knew anything about speaking in tongues and stuff like that.

DR-LILY: I've heard of it.

MICHAEL91773: Do all Fundamentalists do that? You'd think I would have run into it before now. Giselle claims it's a gift from God, a special miracle for praying right from your soul, bypassing your mind.

DR-LILY: A religion that bypasses the mind . . . who would have imagined?

MICHAEL91773: Stop it. Giselle has never said a bad word about science, or about you, even though some of the parents still blame *you* for the riot. At first she did, too, but not anymore, not Giselle. She's very inquisitive when we talk about science, and, unlike you, she's very meek.

DR-LILY: Ah, she's humble. A virtue to swell with pride over.

MICHAEL91773: You're impossible.

DR-LILY: No, no, I admire humility. It teaches you self-contempt, and that's the first step on the time-honored Christian path toward contempt of others.

MICHAEL91773: You're one to talk, Lillian. Sometimes you can be the meanest person I know.

DR-LILY: They're Pentecostals, Mikey. A special breed of Fundamentalists. They speak in tongues, deliver prophesies, hear God's voice, and heal the sick for tax-free donations. You're at the heart of hardcore, among people who keep themselves safe from any truth not already familiar to them through their Scriptures. You're not invited there so that they can listen to you. You're invited to hear what *they* have to say.

MICHAEL91773: That's the word, Pentecostal! It was on the church sign. Weird word.

DR-LILY: It comes from the Jewish Feast of Pentecost. The day the Holy Spirit descended on the twelve Apostles and compelled them to preach to a multinational crowd in languages the Apostles had never learned. It was forty days after the Big Guy got himself resurrected and ascended on up into heaven. Mikey my heart, my sweet, my best friend. I'm not the smartest, meanest person you know. You're confusing me with your parents, or mine. I'm just being protective. Be careful with them. Be careful with this woman. Don't get all swooned away. She has deeper motivations than just getting a cute date for Saturday nights.

MICHAEL91773: That's enough. Damn it, Lillian, that's enough. Don't say anything else about her. You only met her once, and it wasn't under the best circumstances. Stop telling me the motivations of a woman you don't even know!

DR-LILY: Uh oh. You've got it bad, don't you?

MICHAEL91773: I like her a lot. I don't want to hear you . . . to *read* you typing nasty things about her.

DR-LILY: I thought you liked me, too.

MICHAEL91773: I do like you, Lillian. Stop being nasty.

DR-LILY: You're supposed to care about me, Mikey.

MICHAEL91773: I do! You're my Cousin, forever.

DR-LILY: You know what I mean. You know exactly what I mean.

MICHAEL91773: Don't bring this up.

DR-LILY: Don't bring it up? I don't have to bring it up. It's always there. It's a part of us. How can you keep living as if it weren't?

DR-LILY: Why don't you have an answer for that?

DR-LILY: Why can't we ever talk about it?

DR-LILY: Michael?

DR-LILY: Michael?

DR-LILY: Mikey?

—END OF IRC CHAT LOG—

—17—

Greetings to my kind, the No-Flesh Asarkos,

Let me tell you of marvels. Let me proclaim to you mysteries of the flesh, and mysteries of ourselves.

The chariot of Blastus contained three occupants: Blastus, of course; another man vaguely familiar to me, a Jew; and a citizen of Antioch, a doctor. They dismounted quickly, but slowed when they heard Judah's lamenting wail. Blastus knew in an instant that his great effort had failed, and he lowered his head.

The Antiochan physician stood his ground, appearing uncomfortable and no doubt feeling, of a sudden, entirely unneeded. But the Jew moved quickly to where Judah stood.

"She has gone?" the Jew asked Judah.

Judah's lamentations ceased, and the first of my friends here on this planet nodded his head weakly. He lifted his face to behold his newly arrived countryman, then fell to his knees, grabbing and kissing the Jew's hand.

I spoke softly to Luke, crouching to the ground to be closer to his ear. "I know this man whom Judah honors."

"Yes," Luke said without feeling or enthusiasm. "That is Thomas, the Twin. You and I have seen him, but never spoken with him. He is one of the first followers of the Jew named Jesus. An Apostle, their group would call him."

I remembered now with the mind of Saul. Thomas was always in the crowds that accompanied the Christ, a quiet man who asked fewer questions of the Master than the others would. His twin brother, named Caleb, had disowned Thomas as a heretic for following the Nazarene. I, as Saul, had hoped to use Caleb the brother as a plant within the group; my intrigues were fruitless, for Caleb was devout to the philosophies of the Sadducees.

Thomas the Twin boldly crouched and entered the tent of Esther without Judah's invitation. He emerged moments later. There was great concern on his face. "If the others were here, if it were anyone other than me," he said to Judah, not finishing his statement.

When he saw me, the concern on his face vanished, replaced by shock. "Glory to God," he said. He approached me. "Praise and glory to the name of the Lord."

He fell to his knees, and in a manner similar to Judah's honorific greeting to him, Thomas took my hand and kissed it. He looked up at me, and his eyes were very wide. "I cannot understand. So many questions. You! But the questions will wait, and you cannot. Whom would you save?"

The last of what he said was whispered hurriedly, and only Luke and I could hear it. I was confused, but discerned the need to respond in similar hushed tones. "What are you saying, Didumos?" I asked him, using the Greek word for "twin."

"She is not dead! She is only sleeping." There was great urgency to his whisper. "But she will be dead soon. You have only a few moments to do what your people do. Still, you must decide, for the husband is ready as well. Whom would you save?"

I looked to Luke, hoping for some help, some explanation. If there can be such a thing as curious apathy, that would describe the expression Luke returned. One of his hands played with the fabric of his mantle, the hem of which was bunched without dignity about his knees. His other hand innocuously twirled a braid of his long, dark hair. His eyes studied me with bland interest.

"The husband is ready for your hands," Thomas said. "And of course the wife is ready, but we will lose the moment quickly. Save her, and you will lose him for certain. Save him, and there will not be time to save the wife as well."

The barrage of words made me dizzy. I am not accustomed to being befuddled, although my days here on this planet have been training me well for that state. I composed myself. "Is Judah in danger of dying?" I asked.

"No," said Thomas, still kneeling, "but he is as ready for salvation as any man ever was."

I have mentioned it before. I love the wife of Judah.

"If he is safe, then I would save the woman," I said to Thomas. "Tell me what to do."

Thomas rose to his feet, still grasping my hand. "Come," he said.

Here is how my friend Judah would tell the tale. I asked him to recite it, now, tonight, while events are still new in his mind. He tells my own tale of salvation well; I would have him likewise fashion words for Esther's salvation.

"We were traveling the wastelands to Antioch," says Judah, "filled with fear at the threats and admonitions leveled against us by the Jews and the Gentiles of Damascus. The hardships of the past days and of the journey north weighed heavily upon Esther, the beloved wife of Judah, she who bears the name of the great Hebrew Queen for whom Jews still celebrate the Feast of Purim. Esther took ill, and our group was forced to stop until such time as she should recover strength.

"But she did not recover. So Blastus the Roman, who traveled with us, was moved by the spirit of the Lord to race in a single day to Antioch, still several days' journey away. Strengthened by an angel of the Lord, Blastus covered the distance in a time possible for no man, and returned the same day with Thomas, an Apostle of our Lord and Messiah Jesus. But by that time, Esther, wife of Judah, had died.

"Thomas Didumos said unto Paul of Tarsus, 'The woman is not dead, she is only asleep.' And Paul, with Luke and Thomas, entered the tent to speak to the body of Esther in the name of the Lord Jesus.

"And there came a great wind and blinding light, and those outside the tent were filled with awe and wonder. Paul commanded, 'Esther, rise in the name of the Savior Jesus Christ.' And he came from the tent, escorting the wife of Judah, who had been brought back to life by the power of the holy spirit.

"The husband of Esther rejoiced with songs of thanksgiving unto the Lord. Blastus the Roman, for his part, trembled with joy that his efforts had not been in vain, and that the God of Israel had showed forth such great marvels on that day."

—

"I did not tremble," Blastus insisted, his voice unsure and shaking from the exhaustion brought about by the day's mission.

"Your story fails to mention Trophimos, our new physician friend from Antioch," Luke said.

"He did nothing," said Judah, who was filled with greater joy than I had seen in any Sarkate since the day I came here. "But I am most pleased to welcome him into our midst," Judah added, perhaps sensing possible offense in his words.

"You do not mention the horse," Luke said. He did not seem happy with the way Judah worded the account.

"The horse?" Judah laughed. "Such a wondrous marvel performed by the Lord, and you wish to record the dying of a chariot's horse?" The awakening of Judah's happiness seemed to also awaken the congenial goading Luke often gave him. Judah's joy would not be hampered, though; and Luke's goading, I could plainly see, was without its fuller, previous force.

The horse that had sped the chariot to us fell dead suddenly, collapsing at the same time Esther arose from death. Its carcass still rests a score of steps from our evening fire. Great scales have encrusted the dead beast's eyes. I do not know whether they grew there before it died, or after.

"You will let him tell his history in this manner?" Luke asked me. "With so many critical omissions, and dubious details added, attributing forces at work to the God of the Jews?"

"And to the Lord Jesus Christ!" Judah proclaimed.

Judah's telling had, in fact, left out many details. How Thomas had directed me to lay hands upon the dead woman. How he had forced me to look into her eyes directly and speak to her. How her body had spasmed, and how she gasped a breath, causing Luke to cry out in shock. How she burst forth in words, a language called Akkadian, an older dialect of the Babylonians, enemies of my friends the Jews, and how she shouted in that tongue, "We seek the One who seeks The Ten Who Are Missing!"

More details: how Luke, first and foremost a dedicated man of medicine, overcame his shock. Great encrustations, great scales, began immediately forming over the eyes of the again-living Esther, and Luke applied a charism, the selfsame oils he had applied to my own scaled eyes. He had them already assembled and at hand, as if he had expected this. Yet his demeanor was that of a man who had not expected it at all, prepared in spite of unbelief. Esther's scales withered and fell away in an instant, causing Luke again to gasp in astonishment.

Details: how Esther fell silent again, staring helplessly past us, unfeeling. How Luke administered his medicinal liquid, first to her lips, then past them, gently rubbing Esther's throat to make her swallow. How she convulsed from that liquid; how she gasped, how her eyes filled with fright; and then upon seeing me, how she jerked forward and wrapped her arms around me, the fullness of her chest pressed to mine, separated by the thin, negligible fabrics that the Sarkate in modesty wear.

How Thomas said to Luke, "You, then, understand"; how Luke said to Thomas, "I have ideas. But I understand nothing at all."

As Luke and Judah continue to argue across the fire about how this story should be told, the wife of Judah rests beside my Jewish friend. She sits with the men tonight. Judah will not let her from his sight, all Hebrew customs and propriety thrown away in the face of such wonders as today has revealed. He clasps her hand very tightly, right in the full view of us all.

He has her hands, but I hold her eyes. This is Esther, but it also is not. Another Asarkos, another of my race, stares back at me, so many questions in those eyes, and too many Sarkate about us for me to answer them, or to ask questions of my own.

My flesh is filled with great lust for the body inhabited by my bodiless kinsman. My heart is filled with jealously that the woman's body is owned by my dear friend Judah. My mind would have answers; my flesh would have her flesh.

I would speak more with Thomas, who has remained quiet since this miracle. I would know what he knows.

My meditations, and my hold on the eyes of Esther, are broken by a friendly shove from Luke. "What do you say?" Luke demands. "Will you let him turn this into yet another Jewish faith tale, assaulting the story's accuracy?"

Is there challenge in Luke's tone? Is there an insistence that I improve the retelling by adding information only he, Thomas, and I share?

"That is how my friend Judah tells the tale," I say. "I see no reason to doubt any of the data Judah has given us."

I hear the scurrying of nighttime scavengers picking at the carcass of our dead horse. I am determined to hear Thomas's thoughts on the horse, as well. And my determination shall get me what I want, however troublesome the answers may be.

Yours from among the Sarkate,
Paul of Tarsus

FROM: Lillian.Uberland@rsi.edu
RECEIVED BY: [mail unsent]

Kiss-Kiss, Cousin,

Im not going to send you ths one. I promised myself that im not going to, because you won't call me back. You know, yu could call back. Ive left you three messagesw, and you damn well know it. I have to write to you but i'm not going to send it so there.

I'm a little drunk, anyway. I f sent it and you called, It wouldn't be a very good thing. you shouldn't read it anyway, because Im going to talk aout what you don't want me to.

I love you. Im four years older thaen you and i feel like you taght me about sex. I was a virgin when we first made love, Mikey, just like you, and I should mention that I'm not so happy about you being with that woman. Its got nothing to do with science or with religion or with me being arrogant or mouthy, its abotu how I feel about you. You saved my life, you know? You saved me life because I coulodn't have gone on one more minute in that damn family, with my Mom and everything that, you know. And your Dad. It could be worse they could have been child molesters or something more awful than they were, but tey probably were just as bad when you think about it. Theyre so intelligent, aren't they. And they demanded that we be brilliant too, that anything less then straight A-s and a PHD would be such a shame. And remember how we would have to take accelerated courses every summer? They wondered why we never had friend. Well, we didn't have a faculty to force to come to our houses to dinner like they had. Nobody dependded on us for their jobs or their tenure. Screw them. Screw them for all being so smart and so important, and did you hear that now that your Dad's dead they're going to name the library after him? Makes you wonder who its named after now, and how whoever's it is family feels about their smart person being replaced by an even smarter one.

I didn't want to talk about that. I wanted to say I wazs sorry, and that i shouldn't have been so mean about

Stop. I cant even remember what I call the little girl. Her mother, what I said about her mother. That your dating.

Please don't be mad at me/ I don't kniw what I'd do without you. I know I'm not really worth loving and that I'm domineering. That's why you like gisele, isn't it? Because she's submissive to men, just the way her bible teaches her to be, even though your'e not a beliver and even though your're a scientist. science techer. Now, to ME she wasn't nice or submissive. She was nasty to me, and you're right I'm one to talk. POlease don't hate me, Mikey. I love you.

God. I fell asleep at the keyboard and woke up scared that I sent you this, because I'm not goin g to . Excuse me for a second. All right, I' back. It's chablis, the real nasty jug stuff that's sells for eight bucks a gallon. I'm using my big wine glasses.

I didn't get to go to my Senior Prom. Know why? Mom said no extra activities becuase I was going to get a "B" in my "Home and Careers" class/ Home and careers!!! Not math not english not science, especially not science. And you know, the grades weren' even out yet. Mom CALLED my teachers, looking for any problems she could find, and as soon as she did she had her punshment all read y for me. God I screamed at her and yelled and screamed.

But you know what? I wasnt goign to go to the Prom anyway.

Mikey, nobdy asked me to go. Nobody. at all.

"Mousy Girl." That's it. I looked back at what i wrote, caught the typos, and remembers her name. That's what I call her.

When you came to college to visit me, you were just a freshman in high school, and i was a Freshman too at college. Here's something wierd. I wasn't ashamed about making love to you becaquse you were my cousin. I was ashamed of it because your so young. Fou8fr years! It does-n't seem like anything now, but it menas a hell of a lot more when youre in your teens. But how you made love! You remember? Your Dad and mom had one goal for you: utter perfection, more P.hds. than they had, combined, and perfect scores in high school. Boy was that familiar to me, so when you started crying I knew exactly what you were feeling. I had to hold you, I had to cradel you in my arms, and I think, I really do think, that I had to lose my virginity to you. Have you loose yours to me. Who else is there in the world for us? We were so cut off ferom the other kids. We couldnt go places on weekends. Our parents were living their own failed grabbing at perfection through us. Even family get togethers were spent talking aout the universities everybody taught at and what Chairs they were angling to take over. Fun time was Trivial Pursuit, for which you and I got yelled at whenever we didn't know answers that were sup-posed to be obvious. Yelled at. That one time, you even got sent out of the room. Your dad called you "a bloody half-wit," saying "bloody" because he can't admit he's not Britsh nobility, just another american acadmeme nobody. With a library named after him, now that he's dead. Jolly good job, congrats old man.

You know, I counted. You and I tok cmfort in each others arms sixty-three times over four years. I dont know what possesed me to count. But i can remember each and every one. How you smelled. what parts of your bodty sweat the most when we made love. Once you left behnd a tee-shirt, anjd you know what. To this day I have it, because i loved thye smell of you on it. It doesn't smell like you any more, but just holding it brings back to memory of every time we hzad one another.

We had real love. but we also had guilt. And that's funny, because youd think that real, true love would excuse us from guilt, and protect our consciences from ayn consequences. DOnt you think so. Don;t you?

The last time. When you saisd it was thye last time, and I didn't believfe it. But it was. Than you graduated and jumped into getting your teachers certificate. I fought really hard for us to stay friends. If i cant have you the way I want you, then I will have you as my best and only friend in the whole world. See, i"ll prove it. I did a lot of research on glossolalia for you. I know a lot about speaking in tonguwes now. I'm going to tell you about it in my next email, the one I'll really send instead of this one. if I can remember where I left my notes.

I won't mentioned out past any more,. I promise, Mikey. I'll keep it all in my head, the way I rested my face against your neck, the way your arms held me, how you felt inside me. No more about that, just in my head, and I'l even make it go away from my heads if that's what it takes to keep you as my best and only fried. I love you so much. Remember? How much I love you.

Whops. Fell asleep at the keyboard. I've been dringking a little tonighyt, hope I haven't made an ass of myself. Tomorrow I'll send you a message about what I'm learned about speaking in tongues. I did a little research today, and learned a few intreresting things . . . sorry I'm not putting it in this mail, but I'm going to keep this short. I'm tired as hell, Cuz, and I haven't been feeling myself latekly.

Hey, tell me how things are going with Mousy Girls's mom. We should get together for dinner soon, sweet cheeks! Bring her, I'd like a second chance at getting off on the right foot with her. She sounds sweet. Honest! (God, a couple glasses of wine and i'm feeling loopy. Ii'm gonna rgret this in the A.M!!)

Call me. Ive left you some messages.

Your affectionate cousin,

Doctor Lillian

MAIL SENT: 23:29
RECEIVED BY: MNA@sellenville.edu

—19—

Greetings to my kind, the No-Flesh Asarkos,

The years that have passed since I have written on these pages! The many things we have learned! I have kept these scrolls and everything in them a secret, under lock and key. But Luke, who has read all written here, insists that I finish the tale, writing this story to its completion, that others might know and understand.

I shall pretend that it is again those days long ago, before I understood all.

The city of Antioch has the third largest Sarkate population in the civilized world, surpassed only by Alexandria and Rome. In keeping with the Sarkate obsession with endless sequences of names, the city sits in the region called Phrygia, part of the province of Galatia which in turn is an area defined within the vast empire of Rome, on the planet called the World or Earth. The dauntingly massive southwest gate of the city stands at the height of four Sarkate. We were required to pay an entrance tax, a tribute coin called a *tetradrachm*. Blastus carried such coins. The front of one bears honor to the image and name of Tiberius, the Caesar before the current Caesar; the reverse side shows Augustus, and proclaims him a god of the Romans. So the tax we paid was rendered both unto the Caesars and unto the gods.

Marble busts of the god Augustus adorn either side of the gateway, set atop pedestals at bases supporting two great aqueducts crossing over the city walls. But inside, Antioch immediately ceases to be a Roman city, transforming in a matter of steps into a Greek *polis*. Temples to Greek deities abound, a sea of white stairways leading up to temples in honor of Apollo, of Demeter, even one honoring the under-appreciated Diana.

Blastus, Luke, and I were secured lodgings by Thomas Didumos in the home of Trophimos, the physician who had accompanied Blastus into the wasteland. It seemed a safe enough selection of residence; Trophimos was not the cleverest of the Sarkate, so he did not question us closely about our purposes here. Nor was he inclined to say much of anything to anyone, even of the marvels he had witnessed in the desert. As far as I can tell, he said nothing about us to his wife, who accepted us as guests at her husband's command. He did not introduce us to her by name, as Judah had introduced me to Esther. Instead, he directed her to tend to us, a chore added to her tending of their two small Sarkate children.

Esther and Judah did not lodge with us. Those two Thomas took away, dismissing himself with muttered excuses about needing to take them to a place, in order to meet some people. We assumed he would return for us shortly. But four meals and two days later, when not a word had been heard from the Apostle Thomas, my companion Luke spoke aloud what each of us already knew: "My friends, we have been abandoned."

Blastus nodded, accepting without mockery Luke's declaration of the obvious. He moved to the door. With low tone and little inflection, he said, "I need to pay for the horse we killed. It was borrowed from a local *tribunus*, with the weight of my word as the only collateral."

Luke looked surprised. "You carry enough money on your person to pay the cost of a horse?"

"By the grace of Caligula, I am quite rich."

"But do you think carrying it is wise to do, in a city of half a million strangers?"

Blastus put his fists on his hips and let his elbows jut out. It is a Sarkate trick, one that creates an impression of greater mass. It was a trick Blastus certainly did not require.

"Would you, my tiny Greek doctor, try to take that money from me?"

Luke did not consider long. "Eloquently argued," he said.

Within a short time, Luke, too, excused himself. He left unspoken the purpose of his task. I remained in the home of Trophimos, for the moment more than content to continue my thoughts of the past few days, and my observation of Trophimos's children. Watching them helped me understand the death of our horse, and the resurrection of Esther.

Sarkate children begin very small. Trophimos's youngest, a boy named Oecleus, is at most several months old. Like our own development over the eons, the development of a Sarkate is gradual. They start with nothing, it would appear—no data, no understanding of where or what they are, no grasp of the enormity of existence that has been thrust upon them. Their tiny eyes are squinting and uninterested. At first consideration, one would deem a Sarkate newborn to be little more than an animal; and in truth, I suspect they are just that, despite the horrific protestations such a claim would elicit from my friend Judah. Still, new Sarkate are less lucid than a newborn calf, and remain that way longer than newborn pups.

But the other child gives me pause. That one, a girl whom they have named Pricilla, has been alive for over a year. I have studied the eyes of this older child, and I have found them studying me, studying the mother, studying the environs of the inside of Trophimos's home. This small thing is absorbing data and processing information at a rate that would challenge the best of our Asarkos thinkers. Her infant brother operates in a purely animalistic way, reacting to the input of taste and touch; the sister has added sight and sound, and somewhere in the past months has turned hungry for it. Even her nose is used for the input of smells with certain foods set before her for the first time, although the input method of smelling is used with far less frequency than those of seeing and hearing.

If I tried . . . and I do not say I planned to try this, I was only speculating . . . if I tried to take control of my substance, force it to leave the body of Saul, and project it into the little girl, directly through her eyes, what would I have felt? Even the mature mind of Saul caused me to lose control of much of what I knew, at least for a time. I stared helplessly, just as Esther had, unable to cope with the nature, the content, or the sheer quantity of information that the Sarkate absorb as a matter of course. So how much more crippling would it be to enter the toddling girl? Adult Sarkate have learned to regulate the input they accept. I almost believed that Pricilla, the eyes-hungry little child, could consume half the information in the universe and still want more. She would eat me whole.

No, my joint-dweller in the flesh, the familiar voice from within me said. *My guess is that you would become subordinate to her, just as I am subordinate to you.*

Forgive me, Saul of Tarsus, I told him. When I entered you, I knew not what I was doing.

It was justice. I greatly needed to be suborned.

Yes, I agreed. Your ways were not good ways. Tell me, Saul of Tarsus, did you force me to enter your flesh, or was it my own drive that made me select you, an ambition I secretly desired?

I cannot answer that, because it is not the right question. When a rock tumbles down a hill, does it really have the foot of the hill established as its goal? Or does the hill's foot command, "Come to me, rock, that we might join!"? No, Paul. Some things just happen because they happen. I was ready; you were coming. My eyes beheld you; you came in.

How? I asked. How can it be that simple, and that meaningless?

It was not simple. It is no commonplace thing, I suspect, that one of your kind should casually descend to the face of our Earth. And I said that I was ready. You do not yet grasp what I mean by that. My heart had turned against me on the road to Damascus, finally aghast and filled with self-loathing over the fullness of my efforts against an inconsequential band who followed a dead leader; the folly of my lifetime spent to that empty moment; and the horror of my violations of the laws of God, the laws of Rome, the laws of any decent human city. I came face to face with a life started with righteous zeal, but ending in hatred. I gave up. You could not have entered me otherwise.

Despair, I said. Like Judah at the death of Esther. He, too, was ready to die. I see, then, why Thomas said I had to make a choice.

Yes. That kind of living despair is rare in humanity. I do not think it can come to a man more than once. I do not think it comes to most men at all, at least not before true surrender in the moments that life is ending.

See how much he loved her, I said. Dead to himself while still alive. Who could know? See how much. And she has been given back to him.

She was kept from leaving him. She had given up the will, but not the ghost. It was very close, you know, you saved her in the very last moment. Although I have heard it told that Jesus of Nazareth managed to raise a dead man named Lazarus a full three days after death had been declared.

Jesus himself was restored, I said. Tell me, Saul of Tarsus, was Jesus of Nazareth an Asarkos?

You again ask questions I could not possibly answer.

But do you think he was?

All I can do is wonder along with you. But Paul, companion of my flesh, you need to learn more from Thomas Didumos. You realize that he is an Apostle, one of the group called The Twelve.

I know, I said. And I see plainly that Thomas Didumos knows something of my Asarkos race, though he has no Asarkos dwelling within him.

No, he has no other within him.

Nor does our horse, now deceased.

I feel the anger seething in your bowels, Paul of Tarsus. You think a second Asarkos entered the horse, not knowing where else to turn in this mortal plain. That is why you study the children of this home; to determine what might come to pass in different situations of entering earthly flesh.

One of my kinsmen has been lost, that is my impression. If Thomas Didumos knew an Asarkos was coming, he very well knew two were coming. I could have guided both, one to Esther, one to Judah. He forced me to a false choice.

Remember, Paul, that Thomas had little time. Remember that any anger you feel comes from the part of you that gave you flesh. From me.

An Asarkos can feel anger, I told him. It simply takes a little more time. All you have given me is improved velocity.

Think before you act.

I would find Esther, I said. I would speak with Thomas Didumos.

And then I commanded Saul of Tarsus to silence.

—

Luke returned first. He wore no look of satisfaction, and did not seem pleased with himself.

"They hide well in this city," he told me. We sat eating dates he had purchased from a marketplace in a Jewish area of the city. "I met plenty of people who knew of the Christ-sect Jews, but none who would confess to being followers of The Way. That is what they call themselves in Antioch. The Way."

"You tried, dear friend," I reassured him. "We shall try again in the morning." I broke one of the riper dates into small pieces, and gave two portions to the daughter of Trophimos. The child rubbed the bits over her cheeks before trying to eat them. She looked at me intently the entire time.

"Many have heard of Thomas and the other Apostles, but among the common folk Thomas is no longer called *Didumos* the twin, but *Apistos* the doubter. It seems he was not in the room when the Risen Christ first appeared to the Apostles. He had trouble accepting their claims of a visit by the resurrected rabbi."

"I see," I said. "And since the High Priest's spy, Judas Iscariot, was already dead by then, that would mean The Twelve were really The Ten, wouldn't it?"

Luke was confused by the observation. "I suppose that would be the case, yes. They have since replaced Judas."

"But in the beginning, there were ten frightened men, huddled in a room, suddenly bereft of the leader they hoped would change their world forever. Ten men in utter despair."

Luke made no reply. But from within me, unbidden, the voice of Saul said, *Ah. So there it is.*

We sat quietly for a time. The wife of Trophimos took the girl-child Pricilla away, into one of the two back rooms of the house. She did not seem pleased to have me feeding so many dates to the tiny Sarkate.

After sunset, Trophimos returned from the route of homes he visits to practice his medicines. Luke had stopped speaking with Trophimos about medicines; he disapproved of Trophimos's methodology, an approach that invoked gods as often as it invoked healing herbs. Trophimos embraced the ancient, mystic philosophy that "like cures like"; should there be fever, for example, hot compresses ought to be applied and hot foods administered. The fever was how the gods communicated a need for even more heat. Luke, a devotee of the naturalist Hippocrates, took a decidedly different view: that a thing was cured by whatever cured it, and that philosophies about the essence of man and the will of gods had little to do with what worked. The two argued their first evening together, without any of the cordiality Luke afforded Judah in similar disagreements. Luke quickly grew frustrated with Trophimos; even I, who know little of medicines, was struck by the Antiochan's stubbornness, illiteracy, and slowness of wit.

Blastus returned soon after Trophimos. He sat with us without speaking, taking several of Luke's dates, a handful of figs, and a serving of the barley cakes provided by Trophimos's wife. When I poured Blastus a bowl of wine, I asked what news he brought back with him.

"I have paid for the horse," Blastus told us. Then, without further explanation, he began to weep. His shoulders jerked from his sobs. He kept eating his barley cakes and would not look up, but I saw a tear fall and make ripples in the wine bowl set before him.

Much later, well after all lamps had been extinguished, Blastus was willing to speak aloud into the darkness of Trophimos's home. "I have learned a thing I was not meant to know," he said to the darkness. "I spied upon a messenger from the west, not realizing what I would discover. Gaius Caligula has been assassinated. Caesar is dead, and tonight there is no emperor in Rome."

Luke tells me that one of the elements of style in the telling of stories is a device called "suspense." Suspense, briefly, is the withholding of further information at a point when data have just started to become interesting. I employ that technique now, although I find it difficult, since I know precisely how this story ends. But I write for the ones who do not yet know, and Luke encourages me to cast these events in the order they happened, that others might learn as I learned.

So I continue as one still experiencing the tale.

Blastus fell asleep without further discussion of the matter he raised. I, too, needed sleep, my dear Asarkos brethren who dwell beyond this world. I needed energy, because the next day, I planned to drag the Apostles from their hiding places.

Yours from among the Sarkate,
Paul of Tarsus

−20−

SENT BY: Lillian.Uberland@rsi.edu

RECEIVED BY: MNA@sellenville.edu

Kiss-Kiss, Cousin,

Hey, I've left you a few messages and sent you some emails. Have you disappeared from the face of the Earth? Have you decided I'm not worth talking to? Have you forgotten that I'll torment you forever, that there's no hope of getting rid of me, so you might as well yield?

Just kidding, Mikey sweet, just kidding. What I'd really like to know is when you're scheduled to give your evolution talk at that church. If it's okay with you, I'd like to sit quietly in the back and listen to what you tell them. Honest, I won't make a peep. I'll come in disguise if you want.

I found a sticky note to myself that I stuck on my computer monitor, reminding me to write you some of the things I've learned about "speaking in tongues." I also had a note that I wanted to invite you and Giselle to dinner next week. Bring Mousy Girl, too! I promise to be charming, just as long as you write me back and tell me what day's good for the three of you.

Now, on to glossolalia: "speaking in tongues" seems to have started in the early church, and has never quite disappeared in the centuries since. You'll notice I say "seems to," because spontaneous talking or praying in an unknown language can be found in any number of primitive religions around the world. Usually it pops up in the most frenzied rituals, after the shaman or preacher or witch doctor has whipped the faithful into an ecstatic, almost self-hypnotic state.

Oddly, frenzy isn't what happens in most Pentecostal-Fundie churches. It *can* happen, but your typical Christian glossolalist can turn "speaking in tongues" on and off without much thought or emotion. It seems that once they've learned how to do it, it comes as naturally as a real language.

That, of course, brings us to the question: is it a real language? Your new girlie-friend told you that when her Fundies "speak in tongues," they're speaking in the languages of man or of angels. But I've checked the research, Mikey. Not a single Christian speaker of tongues has ever been recorded speaking a foreign language they've never learned. Not one. Even more disappointing for your followers of Christ is that the only seemingly verified case of someone speaking spontaneously in a foreign language occurred with a *Jewish* woman, one who it's reported never learned or had even heard Swedish, but who burst out one day speaking it fluently.

And trust me. She said nothing even remotely similar to, "Ye must call upon the name of the Lord Jesus Christ to be saved." Bummer for the born-agains, huh?

The readings I plodded through (on your behalf, because you asked me too, my dearest friend) showed that even Christians can't decide what "speaking in tongues" is. When their Holy Book first talks about it in the "Acts of the Apostles," it isn't even considered a miracle of speaking. It's a miracle of listening, with everyone in the crowd *understanding* what the Apostles were preaching, hearing it in their own tongues.

Later on in the New Testament, St. Paul the Apostle writes to the Corinthians, and seems to acknowledge that the Christians in that church have a gift for praying in other languages. He even says, "I thank God that I speak in more tongues than any of you." But, man, does Paul lay into them for *using* that "gift" in their churches! He orders them not to pray in tongues unless there's someone else around to interpret what's being said. He calls speaking in tongues a "lesser gift" of God. He tells them he'd rather speak five intelligible words to them than ten thousand words of gibberish. He says that when they babble in tongues, their "spirits" are praying but their minds are doing nothing . . . and he demands to know what good that could possibly be.

For being such a nifty gift, this glossolalia thing sure gets dissed by that St. Paul guy. I'm wondering whether your Fundie friends take him seriously, considering he wrote about half the books in their New Testament. Me, I think I could grow to like St. Paul; anyone who demands that Christians use their minds is okay in my book.

Which is, of course, the Book of Science. Enough Bible chatter; let me talk about glossolalia in the language *I* understand best.

—

"This will be easy!" I told myself. "I'll hop on the Internet, find a quick discussion about how humans evolved to be able to use language, dash off a quick note to Mikey, and be done with the research."

I hereby advise you, as one who has been there, *not* to search the Internet for discussions of how language popped its way into the evolution flow. It's not that there isn't any information out there; quite the opposite, there's too much, and once you've stayed up all night wading through it, you'll come to the conclusion that we have no idea how language first started.

Sure, we know how it changed over *time* . . . how the prehistoric utterance "Grog want girl now!" finessed itself into, "Hello, my dear, would you care to dine with me this evening?" And we even have guesses about where the first words came from: imitations of animal and natural sounds, exclamations of pain, all that. But how we became biologically capable of using language? It almost seems as if that area's been talked about more by *non*-scientists than by real professionals.

Take, for example, the case of the world's most famous living linguist, who shall remain nameless. You may not know this linguist *as* a linguist, since said individual has since used his prominence to become an outspokesman in the fields of culture and government, using minor fame to legitimize what he has to say about *any* topic. This gentleman linguist, without any background in the biological sciences, declared that human brains contain a "universal grammar," and that infants pick up language thanks to a Language Acquisition Device in their heads. This concept has become such a staple of linguistics that the abbreviation LAD is tossed around as if it really represented a physical *thing*.

So I ask, where in the brain is this Language Acquisition Device? Is it in Broca's Area? Wernike's Area? Is it in the right lobe of left-hand speakers, or is it a neural network that stretches throughout both lobes of the brain? LAD is talked about with such certainty, I'm sure *some* linguist somewhere has actually discovered it, probably by dissecting a fellow linguist's brain during casual conversation.

Don't get me wrong; I have no problem with non-scientists crafting hypotheses related to the physical sciences. But Step Number Two in that little exercise should probably be getting a real scientist involved, just to test things out, no? Many linguists, with no proof whatsoever, have completely embraced this LAD hypothesis and treat it as if it's a fact. They use it as a starting point for even more complex linguistic theories.

So, stunned, I have to ask: What gives with the linguists?

Here's advice from a camp I don't usually quote (or at least *didn't* usually quote, until you, Mikey sweet, got all caught up with Creationists). Linguists would do well to listen to the words of Jesus of Nazareth: that a house built on a flimsy foundation of sand is gonna collapse.

Because if whole theories can be developed based on a passing notion that has no solid evidence behind it, what's next for human knowledge? Do we merge the LAD "universal grammar" hypothesis with Carl Jung's "universal spirit of mankind" philosophy, and conclude that all humans have *all* languages pre-coded inside their heads? Hey, why not? Then let's throw on top of that your Fundie friends' belief in glossolalia, and claim that the coming of the Holy Spirit unlocks innate languages already in our brains. That, in turn, would lead to a Fundamentalist movement having glossolalia taught in public school Foreign Language courses, with physical practice of tongues-speaking required in the curriculum for Gym class.

Don't snicker. You think religion wouldn't move in to control even such mundane things as those? I'll prove you wrong. Remember learning in English class (you know, back when they taught grammar) that you should never split an infinitive?

"To go boldly" was right; "to boldly go" was wrong.

But Cousin, there's absolutely no reason English should have that rule. It came about because Latin infinitives are a single word: *ire,* to go, *libere,* boldly, making it impossible for infinitives to split. Since Latin was a far, far holier language than English . . . ask any Pope . . . the language rules of the Romans outweighed the common sense of the Anglos. Infinitive-splitters were told to (promptly) get lost, and to this day we have a grammar rule based not on language, but on a religious faith. Thank you very much, children of God.

So when supposedly rational people like well-known linguists drive theories like LAD, backing up their claims with fame instead of with evidence, it really pisses me off. I spend hours and hours in my fly lab *confirming* things about *Drosophila* genetics already thought to be true; meanwhile, "famous" people get mass-media coverage for every unsubstantiated brain fart they produce.

That reminds me: still no progress on those fruit-fly eye scales. Dr. Kairns thinks I'm wasting too much time on it, and I think he might be right. It's so bad, I'm even dreaming about my flies now. Two nights ago, I dreamed that my scaly-eyes were flying in a perfect circle around my head, singing the Our Father in Latin. I am not making this up. I think I'm in serious need of a mental break.

Which, incidentally, I could get through spending a quiet, pleasant evening dining with you, Giselle, and Mousy. Please, Mikey? I swear I've adopted a new attitude. I promise you that. Look, I've even gotten all the way through an email using the words "tongue" and "linguist" without cracking a single dirty joke or making any provocative innuendoes. Isn't that proof enough?

I miss you, Michael.

Your affectionate cousin,

Doctor Lillian

—21—

Greetings to my kind, the No-Flesh Asarkos,

The central plaza of Damascus had impressed me, but it could not compare with the market of Antioch. Denizens of a hundred countries pushed through the open-air square, with tents and awnings in dozens of hues and shades demarcating the boundaries of temporary shops. Cookwaresmen, potscrafters, herdsmen, fowlers, moneychangers, weavers of tents, sewers of robes, fabricsmen, fruitsmen, meatsmen of animal flesh both permitted and forbidden by the Law of the Jews, harlots assertive, harlots demure, spicemen from the mysterious east, darkmen of the south with exotic animals from lands unknown, and historians whose tales improved with each denarius, shekel, or handbag of raisins proffered by a listener.

And there were preachers of every conceivable faith.

"He is still very sullen," Luke whispered to me. I nearly lost his words to the noise of the crowd. "It's difficult to understand. By all accounts, Caligula was a madman, and Rome is better for his death."

"I do not advise saying that much louder," I cautioned. "The death of which you speak is not public knowledge. Rome would wish to announce a successor at the same time she announces the first's untimely passing. That allows a more orderly transition. We know well that order is the true deity of Rome, worshipped by all her best citizens."

Luke looked around, now nervous. Antioch hosts the largest Roman military garrison in the empire. Their numbers among the crowd were very noticeable this morning.

Blastus halted his trek through the crowd, allowing us to catch up. "Where should this happen?" he asked me.

"Where should what happen?" Luke asked. "Have you two been conspiring without me?"

"We have made an entire career of it," Blastus said.

"Intrigue is what we do well, Blastus and I." No one in the crowd took notice of us, but it was best to be safe. "From this point forward, you should follow well behind us, Blastus. Give no appearance that there is any association between you and me."

"Which wall of prophets will you join?" Blastus asked.

I considered. The outer fringes of the bazaar were lined with the myriad, colorful spokesmen of religions east and west, and a handful of drably robed Hebrews were scattered among them, proclaiming the coming Day of the Lord. "I do not care for the competition of the walls," I told Blastus. "I shall preach from that north-central fountain. It will allow the largest crowd, and I fully intend to attract the largest crowd."

Luke grabbed the sleeve of my overcoat. "You are going to preach?"

"Of course," I told him. "That is my job as a rabbi. I am a Pharisee among Pharisees, and I have neglected my work of late. These people need to hear of the Risen Christ, and of how I met him on the road to Damascus."

Luke released me. "My only consolation is that no one will listen," he said. "Else I would beg to join Blastus in his arduous task of appearing to have no association with you."

"They will listen." My voice made clear that I would entertain no doubts from Luke. "With Blastus's forgiveness, I swear they will listen."

Sarkate preachers rarely use material amenities when addressing a crowd. This is because a typical preacher desires there to be no distractions from the presence, person, and charisma of the preacher himself. It is not a bad tactic, I suppose; but in this marketplace, with so many gods and their so many messages, I had no desire to blend in with the typical preachers. I stood upon the edge of the north-central fountain, where it is not customary for the preachermen to stand. I drew a scroll from my robes and unrolled it; though it was blank, I studied it as if it were a message of vital import. And then I pretended to read from it, pronouncing carefully and loudly each syllable.

In Antioch, it is in a preacher's better interests to preach in Latin or Greek, the two tongues likely to be spoken as secondary languages by the multitude of nations present. Those were the languages I studiously ignored.

In an Asian tongue known to the spice traders of the Indias, I declared, "Hear me, oh visitors of Antioch. Be it known today that Gaius Julius Caesar Germanicus, he who is called Caligula, Emperor of great and glorious Rome, has been killed at the hands of his own people!"

I did not attract immediate attention. A pair of spicemen stopped and took notice.

"Hear me, oh visitors of Antioch. Be it known today that Gaius Julius Caesar Germanicus, he who is called Caligula, Emperor of great and glorious Rome, has been killed at the hands of his own people!" This time I spoke to the Parthians in their tongue. I had spotted them close by, identifying them by their distinctive hair tassels and lack of headdress.

"Gaius Julius Caesar Germanicus, he who is called Caligula, Emperor of great and glorious Rome, has been killed at the hands of his own people!" Now speaking to the Elamites. And after that to the Medes. Then to the Pamphylians, then the Egyptians, then the Ethiopes, whereupon I began the cycle anew and spoke to the spicemen of Asia, repeating the same message. I allowed the wisdom of Saul of

Tarsus to guide me. I cannot remember how many times I repeated the words, but after many cycles the crowd stood a dozen men deep, arranged in a large oval about the north-central fountain. They faced me, speaking in whispers to their kinsmen, waiting for me to return to my message in their own tongue. There were well over three hundred paying me heed.

Not enough, Saul of Tarsus chided me. *I attracted this many as a newly bearded youngster on the Temple grounds in Jerusalem.*

He was the one with experience at this. So I made pretense of unrolling my scroll further and declared the death of Caesar again, now to the Cyrenes, now to their Lybian neighbors, now to Persians, now to the barbarians of Gaul, should there be any in the crowd, once even to the long-dead Hittite race, lest their memory be forgotten (this earned me light scorn from Saul), and again I recited my multi-language cycles to all assembled. Still the crowd grew. The Roman soldiery took notice, but the multitude was packed in tight to hear if it were true that Caesar had been killed, and they had completed their circle around my fountain.

I found Luke in the crowd. He studied me, cautious, as if I were an anomaly intruding into the schemata of his sciences. I did not see Blastus. Blastus was not meant to be seen.

"What message do you give these people?" The question was shouted in Latin, and I picked out the military tribune far back in the mob.

"Hear, oh visitors to Antioch," I said in crisp, precise Latin, earning the ear of the entire crowd now, and the soldiers as well, "hear that Gaius Caligula Caesar has been murdered!"

I had expected an explosion of excitement by the crowd, now that the message had been declared in the universal tongue. The abrupt silence, even to the point of abated breathing, disoriented me. Further, I realized that several Roman soldiers were closer than I had thought, and two of them rushed toward me now, hands raised to strike me. I felt panic; Saul of Tarsus, though, had readied my tongue.

"I say to you today, speaking as a citizen of the great Roman Empire, that Caligula has been struck down." The soldiers stayed themselves; without a trial or the direction of their proconsul, they were forbidden by law from striking a Roman citizen. "Were I but a citizen and nothing more, that would suffice to trouble my spirit. But these events touch me more deeply than you realize, for I am not only a citizen, but am counselor and courtier to Herod Agrippa, the prince of the Tetrarchy by appointment of Rome herself. And further, as you might surmise, I am a Jew, a kinsman of Herod, and a believer of a faith so strict that no witness can stand alone. We adhere to a law which demands the testimony of more than one voice; so for my Judean kinsmen, and for other races and beliefs, I call upon you, honorable *tribunus militares*, to confirm the news we must share with the world today!"

I held a beseeching hand out to the tribune who had earlier made his demand of me. The two soldiers who had rushed me now disappeared quietly into the crowd. I was a citizen, a counselor to Herod, a Tetrarchan courtier, and now a witness in conversation with an officer. Such matters were well beyond the tastes of simple foot soldiers.

My audience fixed its attention on the tribune. I could tell from the tribune's hesitation that he struggled to determine whether I spoke from an official capacity, and whether this were indeed a proclamation sanctioned by the proconsul or the governor of Antioch. "I do not have . . . I cannot confirm the news you announce today."

"We are lost!" I bellowed. I took back the audience. "Each and every man here today is lost! But we are not left without hope! You may ask yourselves, 'What shall we do without Caesar?' But I tell you, I know of one who is greater than Caesar! I shall tell you today of the new King, the new Lord, the leader of all men who will show the world great power, and teach us of all that is righteous!"

The murmurs rose throughout the crowd as kinsmen told kinsmen who spoke no Latin that I was about to declare the name of Caesar's successor. Even the Roman soldiery whispered among themselves; I realized that they, too, were not certain of the death of Caesar, though apparently they had heard rumors.

Now, and quickly, said Saul of Tarsus. *By now someone is certainly speeding to the governor's palace to confirm your authority.*

"Any leader who is claimed to be greater than Caesar must be proven great indeed. So I ask, will Caesar rise from the dead? Will Gaius Caligula defeat his wounds, and cheat the very grave?"

Even some of the Roman soldiery reacted to that in a way that hinted they hoped it could not be so.

"I speak to you of a man who was likewise put to death by the Romans, but who escaped death and rose again on the third of three days. I speak to you of Jesus of Nazareth, whose followers hide in this very city. You have heard of the followers of The Way, but you have not heard their whole story. It is left to me, a man once called Saul of Tarsus, once the bitterest enemy of the followers of The Way . . . it is left to me to tell you of the great wonders that have occurred in our midst, and how you might share in the glory of the Good News. For in our time, death has been defeated, and the grave has lost its sting . . ."

And I told them. I spoke the same story that the believer Ananias had told me in the house of Judah in Damascus. But I also spoke with the style and authority of Saul, a delicate task of bringing together every shred of evidence available to support my seemingly absurd claims. For the Jews I cited the prophet Isaiah, who wrote of the coming Son of David with sweet eloquence. For the spicemen of the east I talked of their legendary holy man Mithras, finder of life through death, agent of good and foe of Ahriman the satan. For the Greeks I talked of the descent of Theseus to hell and back, a symbol of Christ's mission. The Egyptians I told of Osiris, unjustly slain yet brought to life again. In all I touched on fifteen foreign myths of diverse cultures, assuring each and every listener that those tales all pointed wisely, as symbols of the truth, to Jesus of Nazareth, the Christ of the Jews.

I had no time to move to a sixteenth example. The shining, orderly helmets of the palace guard appeared at the western entrance to the market. I rushed my evangelical call for action with the words, "Therefore, brethren, repent. I thank you." Then I forced myself into the crowd. Luke met me, throwing over my shoulders a brown, hooded cloak that made me look like any other Hebrew rabbi walking in the crowd that day. He led me through the masses, distracting others as he went by stopping and pointing excitedly toward the palace guard, or at times insisting he had spotted the quickly departed preacher, there, heading off to the south. We soon eluded all detection, disappearing from among them while remaining in their midst.

—

"*Ichthus,*" Blastus said, using the Greek word for "fish." "Its letters abbreviate the phrase 'Jesus Christ, Son of God, Savior.'"

Luke recited the Greek, using his fingers as if counting. "*Iesous Christos, Theou Uios, Soter.* Yes. That is a 'fish.'"

"They etch a fish symbol over the doorways of their meeting places. It is a secret sign to other followers of The Way."

Blastus's role in the preceding effort is simple in the telling, but was taxing in the physical endurance and espionage entailed. At the moment I changed my proclamation from a discussion of the death of Caesar to the message of the Risen Christ, Blastus studied the reactions of listeners. Those who showed minor curiosity or, likewise, minor annoyance at my change of theme, he discounted. Listeners who looked startled, or who showed too much interest, or who reacted in any other way that indicated pre-knowledge of my grand theme of the Christ, those listeners he noted and watched. It came to pass as we hoped; several of the startled listeners made haste away from the crowd. Just as the Romans had their informants who ran to the governor's palace to notify authorities of my words about Caesar, so the followers of The Way had informers bent on notifying believers of my words about Christ.

We had hoped Blastus would track two or three of them to their hiding places. He tracked eight, four of whom made haste to the same location at different times. Antioch is no small city, and the running to and fro would have beaten a lesser man than Blastus. I had ceased being surprised at his stamina, just as he had ceased showing reactions to the wonders and oddities that surround me. He had returned to the emotionless Blastus I knew for years. But looking at him, I could see that something critical was missing. Luke was correct in his assessment of Blastus's despair.

Caligula would not be missed by most; his murderous antics tainted Rome, and his attempt to erect a statue of himself in the very Temple of Jerusalem had made him no friend of the Jews. I think Blastus was not feeling the loss of an emperor as much as he was feeling the loss of Rome herself. Augustus ruled for over three decades; Tiberius ruled well into a third. The murder of Caligula a mere three years and ten months into his reign did not auger well for the stability of the empire.

"Tomorrow is Sabbath," I told my companions. "They are likely to meet on that day for their ritual of breaking bread and sharing wine. I anticipate Apostles being in their midst."

"But the right one?" Luke asked. "How can we be certain that Thomas the Doubter will be among them?"

"I am most eager to meet any Apostle, my friend."

Indeed, I was.

Yours from among the Sarkate,
Paul of Tarsus

—22—

SENT BY: Lillian.Uberland@rsi.edu

RECEIVED BY: MNA@sellenville.edu

Kiss-Kiss, Cousin,

When I keep writing you, even though you never respond anymore, does it make me look desperate?

Well, dear Cousin, I am desperate. I'm not sure if you know what's been going on over here at RSI for the past week; just in case you don't know, I'll fill you in.

About ten times a day. That's how often Dr. Kairns, our department chair and my boss, has to pick up the phone and listen to raving, ranting complaints about me; has to hear loyal believers in Christ telling him I'm a public menace because of last month's riot at your school; has to put up with demands that atheists like me shouldn't be allowed to teach at our American schools; and has to remind those oh-so-bright callers that RSI is a private college, not a public high school. Yesterday he got even more calls than usual. Fifteen! He is not happy. He doesn't like having to let every call bounce over to voicemail. Kairns is the kind of guy who prefers picking up the phone when it rings.

His email is filled with Fundamentalist propaganda, too.

And last night, he got a call on his *home* phone.

It seems people from all over the country are raising a ruckus about my existence, and have decided to fill Dr. Kairns's world with their noise until something is done about me.

So I have to wonder. Why didn't this outcry take place right after the riot? Why is it popping up now, a month and a half after the story hit the national newswires? Well, surprise, surprise: all this activity happens to coincide with the opening of the trial against that Fundamentalist meathead who assaulted you on Creationism Day.

Mikey, my heart, you know how I feel about conspiracy theories and the paranoids who subscribe to them. But there's a teeny, tiny part of me that thinks, Gosh, is the timing of this harassment a little suspicious?

And a part of me that asks, Hey, why didn't Mikey tell me that this trial was finally starting?

And a part that wonders, Shouldn't I have been subpoenaed for testimony in this trial, since I was a direct eyewitness?

And another part . . . yes, love, there are many, many parts of me working overtime these days, and this last one is the angriest of them all . . . a part that demands to know: Who broke into the university fly lab last night, destroyed all my fruit flies, toppled half the equipment, and spray-painted the words "Baal-zebub" on the wall in two-foot high red letters?

All these events could be disconnected, I suppose. Just to be fair, I considered the possibility that hundreds of individuals around the nation were independently moved within their own hearts to call or email my boss. This great awakening started last Tuesday, of its own accord. By coincidence, your email stopped functioning that very same day (probably because of all the national bandwidth being used up by notes to my department chairman), and that's why you couldn't let me know about the trial. In the meantime, the District Attorney who's trying the assault case called Mikey v. Meathead is frantically searching for the file containing my name, address, phone number, and hour-long police statement, too embarrassed to call the state troopers to request another copy. To round things out, some RSI frat boys happened to get good and drunk last night, and one of them said, "Y'know, I really frikkin' hate those *Drosophila melanogaster* things. Let's trash the fly lab and write ancient Hebrew terms on the walls."

I tried hard to believe all those things were separate occurrences. You think I'm being sarcastic, but I'm not. I tried, and for a while I made myself believe it. Ever since you stopped returning my calls and responding to my emails, I've been taking a hard look at myself. Have I become so cold, so skeptical, and so absorbed in scientism that I've grown into a cruel and bitter woman? Has the loneliness of my youth won out? Could it be that my only response to the wonders and marvels of this world is to analyze them, break them apart, weigh, judge, calibrate, and categorize each piece of wonder until I've beaten out of it anything that could be called wonderful? Have I become a sad and pitiable thing, just a shadow of a real human being?

I am very sad these days, Cousin Mike.

My attempt to believe that everything that's been going on is disconnected started to break down early this morning. After we filed the vandalism report with Public Safety, one of my students visited the demolished fly lab, a geeky but congenial freshman named Bernard. He stopped by to help clean things up, and when he saw the graffiti on the wall, he laughed.

"Lord of the fly," he said, pointing at "Baal-zebub."

"It's a name for Satan, isn't it?" I asked him.

"Kind of. But you usually see it as 'Beelzebub,' with two e's, you know? Like in the New Testament. But that spelling there is a lot older, the way it's used in the Old Testament. Kind of like whoever wrote it preferred the ancient Hebrew spelling, and really *wanted* it to say 'Lord of the fly,' just to be sure it was right."

It did seem to be spelled wrong, or at least different from how I thought it should be spelled. I hadn't noticed until he pointed it out. "So,

Bernard, should we tell the police we're looking for vandals who speak ancient Hebrew?"

I think he took me seriously. "Nah, probably not. But you've gotta admit there aren't many people who would know a distinction like that."

"*You* knew a distinction like that," I told him. He got nervous, and I had to reassure him that I didn't think he vandalized the lab. You never saw anyone look so relieved at being exonerated by having their geek-ness recognized, and having their own smartness be the alibi for knowing more than most people do.

A few more students showed up, and by noon we had the place back in order. Even Dr. Kairns pitched in for a while. We'll have to buy some new supplies and a starter batch of virgin and male *Drosophila*.

There's no way to replace my missing notes, of course, but I didn't lose all of them. Just the notebooks on eye-scaling in my mutant-generation batch. Those have vanished.

Hmm. I think, just for kicks, I'll ask if we can keep "Lord of the fly" up there on the wall. Kairns might be favorably disposed to that. He suddenly became far nicer to me today. You see, whoever is doing all this has just screwed up big time. With the phone calls and the emails, Kairns was the victim, the one being annoyed; today it became obvious that I was the victim, too; and suddenly, we're in it together. This little act of vandalism destroyed *his* property in *his* department, and he's been pushed to feeling protective of *his* faculty member, Dr. Lillian Uberland, fellow victim.

Whoops . . . suddenly, my doubts all disappeared! Holy cow! What happened to my dedication to thinking these things were unrelated? Did a little writing on the wall yank me back from the kinder, gentler Lillian I was in danger of becoming? Almost, Mikey. But not quite. The real kicker was this morning's newspaper. I didn't get to read it until after work, thanks to all the chaos I walked into this morning.

But there it was: "School Rioter Cops Plea to Disorderly Conduct."

Disorderly conduct? I had to be reading it wrong. It was out-and-out assault. I saw it with my own eyes! The news stations had footage of him walloping you! But there in the text of the article, you were quoted as saying you'd contributed to the situation with . . . what was it? . . . "verbal abuse, inciting the attacker to a violent reaction." Also quoted: the District Attorney with the misplaced Lillian Uberland files, saying the charge was a fair one given the circumstances, and urging the peaceful citizens of Sellenville to put this unfortunate incident behind them.

Unfortunate incident? Verbal abuse? Mikey, even if the news footage wasn't decisive, I know, I *saw*, I was staring right at you while you pushed through the crowd. You weren't inciting that guy with verbal abuse. You didn't say a damned *thing!* Your eyes were fixed on me, and you didn't even see the thug coming! You, my dear, my heart, my best friend, lied your ass off to the court or to the District Attorney.

Good-bye weepy, sad, benefit-of-the-doubt Lillian; hello, rationalist bitch. Time to employ the scientific principle of "parsimony": reduction of multiple events to the fewest number of required causes. You remember that principle, don't you Mikey? We also call it Ockham's Razor, the rule that you don't need ten or twenty explanations when just one or two will work fine.

So let's take a look at my data, and ask some questions:

1) Who would know the Old Testament vs. New Testament spellings for "Lord of the fly?" Humor me, and pretend it's not my student Bernard.

2) Who would want to keep you from testifying against a Fundie rioter and assailant?

3) Who would rally born agains and Fundies to try to destroy my standing within the RSI faculty, making it inconvenient to have me around or offer me tenure?

4) Who would want to discourage you from contacting me, the one person who keeps you connected to the world of rationalism, evolution, science, and reason?

5) Who have you been dating lately?

Go ahead, get pissed at me. I haven't even given the answer to those questions, and you're already mad, aren't you? All that shows is that you, too, know the answer, and that there's something inside of you that doesn't want me to say it out loud or write it here. So go ahead and get furious. Call me every nasty name you can think of. Wear yourself down over what you think is my unfair accusation. And when the energy is drained out of you and you collapse into a comfy chair, ask yourself, "What other answer could there be?"

Work hard to find that other answer. Let me know what it is, once you find it. In the meantime, my generous invitation for dinner at my place is withdrawn, unless you'd care to come alone.

One answer accounts for almost all my questions. The only one left unanswered is: what on earth would anyone want with all my notes on fruit fly eye scales?

If you can work that into your alternative answer, I'll be happy to accept your explanation and abandon mine. In the meantime, I'll stick with my own hypothesis, and let the eye-scaling-notes thing dangle as a weird, mysterious loose end that might never be explained.

I'd ask you to write back, but I know you won't.

Your affectionate cousin,
Doctor Lillian

—23—

Greetings to my kind, the No-Flesh Asarkos,

The Sarkate imbue ephemeral qualities with near-substantive significance, acting as if what we of the Asarkos would deem a "concept" were really, truly a material "thing." For example, take the notion of "faith." To us, the Asarkos, faith is simply an extrapolation beyond observable data, an assertion like: "Because A is true and B is true, it is very likely that C is true, although I have not yet observed C." Having made that assertion, we the Asarkos would then move to detect evidence of C. "Faith" would be our motivation for investigation, but we would not truly declare C to be a reality until evidence of C was observed. The faith is a conduit to fact, not treated as fact itself.

For the Sarkate, a very different scenario is drawn. The faith itself becomes a thing, as if in and of itself it were evidence of other things not seen, giving substance to what is not yet known. So strong is this bias that religions among the Sarkate quickly move from being a group of matter creatures having faith, to the same group declaring itself a Faith, whereupon the creatures themselves embody the intangible concept and call themselves *The* Faith.

Once *The* Faith is in place, it can become more real than observable reality. Think back several epistles to the tension between my friend Judah and myself, on that day I made the observation that dogs and goats may share a common ancestor. Judah was appalled by the thought, because at some time in the distant past it was important to the forebears of his faith to declare that each creature upon the face of the Earth reproduced according to its own kind. But the assertion is simply false: for give me a Jewish donkey and a Roman horse, and I can make them reproduce, resulting in a new beast, called a mule. It does not matter that the mule cannot reproduce; the creation of a single new animal from two unlike animals clearly shows there are exceptions to Judah's "each according to its kind" rule.

Having only been in two cities and two marketplaces of this world, already I had encountered many manners of beast that share notable similarities, one with the other. The goat, the dog, and the sheep; the horse and the donkey; any and all variety of birds. In the marketplace of Antioch, the darkmen of the south displayed many exotic animals, but what intrigued me most about them was not their differences from beasts known in the mind of Saul, but their striking similarities. Nearly all the exotic creatures with fur and hair walked on four legs, having eyes and ears; but the creatures with feathers strutted about on two legs, and had no ears that I could see. Most intriguing in the display was a creature that did not always walk on all fours, a hairy female beast with a single offspring in her arms, held captive in a wooden cage. In my first moments on this planet, I could very well have mistaken that creature as a variety of Sarkate. I noted few differences between the beast's offspring and the infant child of our host Trophimos.

Judah would have been appalled at these thoughts. He had great faith; reality was hard-pressed to prevail against it.

If you are reading this, my Asarkos brethren, you no doubt notice that I am avoiding discussion of the next day's events. Perhaps it is not so much avoidance as it is circumspection. For I approached that day with great faith, the faith that I would find The Ten Who Are Missing, embodied in the Apostles of Jesus. I did exactly as the Sarkate do: I made my faith *The* Faith that drove me, and I made the Hope so real to myself that I still had trouble, the night that I should have written these words (instead of now, many, many years later) allowing reality to win back my mind.

Our first attempts to uncover the believers were fruitless. Apparently they had moved their unique rituals to the day after Sabbath. So the following day we tried again, resuming our positions on the street called Cyranos to watch the entrance of the fish-marked home most visited by informants for The Way. This time, the observation succeeded. Over a score of visitors, male and female, entered the home, well-spaced in their arrivals, and so casual that if one were not watching carefully, one would not suspect that home held more than two dozen souls. A woman greeted each at the door, kissing first one cheek, then the other, of newly arrived believers. We waited for a time, and no one else entered, indicating that their rituals had begun.

"With so many in attendance, we may be able to enter unnoticed," Luke suggested. Blastus's scowl dismissed the option, and I concurred. The time for subtlety had ended. I led my companions to the door and opened it, walking in freely and without introduction.

Someone had been speaking, but stopped abruptly. I am not certain what I expected to see in the home; perhaps the hierarchical trappings one sees in a synagogue, with the Torah displayed in front, the rabbi leading lessons before the congregants, the men seated on pillows before the rabbi, the women sitting on the floor at the back. Here, instead, I saw two long banquet tables, all in attendance seated about with no one in a superior position. Both tables were filled with wine bowls and bread. No one was standing, and all turned to look at us.

"I seek the Apostles of Christ," I announced.

No one moved for a time. At last a woman stood from her place at the table. She was young, but by no means so young as to be a maiden. "I am Martha of Bethany. You are welcome to my home, and if you are travelers, I will be happy to grant you food and lodging. Right now I meet privately with friends, and I ask that you return after midday for a proper welcome."

I had no patience for having my request brushed aside. "Who is the husband of Martha, that I might ask again to see the Apostles of Christ?"

"I have no husband, sir," she said. "This is my home, and mine alone."

It struck me that I had been speaking too much from the mind of Saul. Romans allowed sole ownership of property by women, and although Martha of Bethany was most certainly a Jewess, she was also a resident of the Roman province Antioch. Still, she spoke with an authority one does not hear outside of royal courts, where women of the palace wield supremacy over common citizens.

As I pondered this and resolved not to allow the biases of Saul to lead me on the last steps of this journey, a man stood from the second table. "Martha, this is not your trouble to be burdened with," he said in Aramaic. I had been addressing them in Greek. "Sir, I am an Apostle of the Lord Jesus Christ, called by the name Simon, and known as the Zealot. There are other Apostles in our midst, Simon who is called Peter, and Levi who is called Matthew." Two more men stood. Simon called Peter seemed more fearful than the other two.

"I—we are—" I could not speak. I wanted to call them liars, frauds claiming to be the Apostles and hiding the true followers. But old memories came back to me, each of their faces as younger men in the group most devoted to Rabbi Jesus. They were the ones they claimed to be, but I could sense in them no Asarkos presence. They were not as Esther was, not carriers of my bodiless brethren.

"We know who you are," Simon the Zealot said, assuming I had stammered in introducing myself. "Saul of Tarsus, who persecutes the followers of The Way."

I could not answer. I had had great faith, great hope. I stood, silent, one who was suddenly lost in the face of reality.

Luke spoke for me. "He who was called Saul is now called Paul of Tarsus. I am Luke, and this is Blastus, each of us with but one name apiece, for which we apologize." Luke looked to me, his eyes holding the expectation that I would take back the discussion. I could not. "Paul of Tarsus is now a follower of the Risen Christ. He is honored to meet the Apostles gathered here, but would most like to meet again with Thomas, who is called the Doubter. The two became acquainted in the deserts south of Antioch."

Simon the Zealot looked surprised. "You were the ones Thomas went to meet in the desert? We were told he had left Antioch, but to my knowledge he has not yet returned." The Apostle named Matthew raised his palms in weak agreement.

"Why were you proclaiming the news of our Lord Jesus Christ in the marketplace?" The Apostle Simon Peter spoke with a fury that stood in contrast to the fearful quivering of his hands. "Did you think we would be deceived by you? You were calling upon Gentiles to believe in the messiah of the Chosen People! Since you cannot *remove* the spirit of Christ from our race, you have decided you must *corrupt* it. You cannot fool us so easily!"

"Yet here we are in your secret gathering place, fool," Blastus said evenly, in Latin. To me, he said, "They speak the truth. It is clear from their faces that they did not know Thomas had returned, or where he is now hiding."

"Sit down," Martha of Bethany told Peter. It was not a command, but neither was it a gentle invitation. Peter sat. Martha approached, taking me by the arm and leading me to the door. "You seek Thomas, but we do not know where he is. Your mission here is done, although I still am happy to give you the evening meal if you visit later this day. You have traveled very far, and I would provide you the comfort a sojourner deserves."

Again, that quickly, we were outside. The faith I had was gone, and the hope I carried was broken.

"You have traveled very, very far," she said, and then closed the door to us.

Blastus had again disappeared from Trophimos's home. After many hours of sitting silently, I said to Luke, "They think I am a killer."

"You are a killer," Luke said, but his voice was not unkind.

"Amongst themselves, they say I am trying to trick them so that I might continue the persecution started by Saul."

Luke finished mixing the poultice he was preparing for Trophimos. He had taken to helping with the man's medicines as a way of paying for our extended visit, and had treated a patient with heat blisters upon our return from Martha's gathering of the believers. "You gave a powerful proclamation of their faith when you spoke in the marketplace," Luke said. "I am certain there are some among the believers who say you are no longer their persecutor."

"And what do you say of me?" I asked.

"I say I am your friend."

"But who do you say that I am?"

Before answering, Luke wrapped the medicinal paste carefully within the folds of a Cilicium cloth I had woven. "My philosophies are by no means Socratic. But there are intriguing passages in the writings of Plato. In one, Socrates says, 'The human soul reasons best when it is untroubled by hearing or sight or pain or any pleasure. The soul reasons best when it says good-bye to the body and, as far as it can, does not commune nor connect with it to reach out to reality.'"

"That is an interesting passage," I said. "Is it supposed to be your answer?"

"I cannot know yet, Paul of Tarsus. Perhaps you will enlighten me as to whether it should be my answer. You can tell me over dinner at the house of Martha of Bethany."

I waved my hand at him. "There is no reason to go. Her invitation was a social politeness only. Her people know nothing that I need to know."

"If it were meant as social politeness, she might have spoken it in a tongue understood by all present."

At first I did not understand what Luke meant. Then I asked, "Was she not speaking Aramaic?"

"At first, but when she walked us to the door, she spoke to you in Ugaritic, the dead language of the Phoenicians."

The implications came to me slowly. I stood, and donned my traveling robe.

Luke, too, prepared to leave. "My friend, you must learn to pay more attention to things like that."

My dear Asarkos brethren, there is something to be said for faith and for hope. And, I add, for love, because, as I am sure you have discerned, behind all my efforts was the love I had for our lost kinsmen, and in particular my newfound love for the woman Esther, of late become one of us. I will acknowledge that of those three, of faith and hope and love, I believe the last to be the greatest.

Yours from among the Sarkate,
Paul of Tarsus

−24−

SENT BY: Lillian.Uberland@rsi.edu
RECEIVED BY: MNA@sellenville.edu

Kiss-Kiss, Cousin,

Wow. Weeks and weeks of not hearing a word from you, and suddenly, boom, a ten-page email. And holy smokes, the topics you cover! You hammer physicists for not understanding that the speed of light is variable, that light's been slowing down over the millennia and that's why we see stars from so many billions of light-years away, even though the Earth is only 10,000 years old. You slam geologists for their carbon-dating techniques, claiming that their flawed approach gives false dates to the fossils we've found. You rip apart archeologists and paleontologists for not understanding that the strata of their finds may have been completely disrupted by a universal flood, thus making the order of discoveries meaningless. You attack paleontologists for not understanding that dinosaurs really lived during the times of humans, citing Scriptural references to a "leviathan" and a "behemoth" as evidence. Scientists in general you disparage because they threaten the moral fabric of civilization, making materialism the guiding force of society and thus opening the doors to atheists, agnostics, humanists, and other abominations. Let me check, did I read that right? Yes, there it is . . . "threaten the moral fabric of civilization." You actually wrote that phrase.

And of course, we evil evolutionary biologists earned the lion's share of your wrath. Most of the last seven pages, by my quick scan.

One thing I couldn't find, though. That line in your email where you said, "Hi, Lillian, how have you been?" I'll answer anyway: fine, thanks.

I'm going to take a really bizarre, going-out-on-a-limb stab here: Mikey has become a Christian, and joined his girlfriend's church with a fervor. Ah, what is this force, this energy, this insanity we call love? Who can know its power? Who can understand its directions, or where it starts, or where it will lead?

Mikey has been saved. Mikey can go to hell. I'm not going to argue with Mikey any longer.

I am tired. You almost had me, you and your new friends. You almost pushed me over the edge, almost forced me into despondency. It didn't work, though. Tell your girlfriend and her cronies that they've failed. I have not been beaten, and they haven't tricked me into living my life in despair.

You know what I think, my formerly dear Cousin? I think they weren't really trying to beat me at all. I think all of this was part of an elaborate plan to get *you*. The more they brought me into it, the more pressure you'd feel, the more torn you'd become over the way of life represented by me, and the Way of God, as represented by your can't-touch-me-till-we're-married sex kitten Giselle. And you know what really disgusts me? That they used not just me . . . me with my predictable behaviors and staunchly atheistic scientism . . . but that they also used their own children, maneuvering them to set you up for the capture. Their children aren't like them yet; I learned that the day Mousy Girl touched my hand and with genuine concern said, "It's all right." I learned that when your boys stood over you during the riot and protected you . . . protected you from the very rioting bastards their own parents had secretly set up to turn Creationism Day into a violent fiasco. Those kids were used. Their children were pawns, just as much as I was.

And to what end? To get you, the evolution teacher of their kids' public school. Now they've got you, got your heart, got you wanting to bed one of their babes. They've got a school district insider, a science teacher who can't really teach their approach to Creationism, but who will no longer emphasize evolution with much conviction. Oh, enough to satisfy the state curriculum, I'm sure. But just enough, and always seasoned with the disclaimer, "Evolution, of course, is only a theory."

What the hell. There are plenty of other topics to cover in a tenth-grade Biology class. Cell structures, photosynthesis, lots of stuff about kingdoms and phyla and species, the chapter on viruses, the whole week spent dissecting fetal pigs. You can probably squeeze evolution into a day or two. Forget that it's the organizing principle of all biology. Forget that sciences like physics, geology, chemistry, almost everything, will have to be thrown out the window if the literal interpretation of your Book of Genesis is true. Because Mikey has a girlfriend. Mikey has a new faith. Mikey's got religion.

Or does he? Because frankly, my former love, your spewing diatribe of ten pages made you sound very much like a person desperate to be right. So desperate, in fact, that you dropped little hints in there, hints that you're terrified. Terrified that maybe you're wrong. Desperate to hear my responses, so that you can create better answers to those who challenge your new approach to science. Every point you made in that email was a little plea for me to answer you, and to give you an argument that you can pick apart.

I'm not going to talk to you about science. Not now, and not ever again. I'm sorry, Mikey, but you are no longer worthy to hear about it from me. Not with the new mindset you've adopted. All you really want now is what your new friends want: to hear what scientists have to say about science, so that you can find its weakness and rip it to shreds for the greater glory of your fringe religion.

And you are a fringe, you know. Roman Catholics and mainstream Protestants have absolutely no problem accepting evolution as a scientific fact. They've been able to adjust their beliefs to fit reality, just as earlier religions eventually got around to coping with an Earth that spun around the sun, despite what the Scriptures claim about that. And just in case your Fundamentalist friends chuckle and explain that Catholics and mainstream Protestants aren't *real* Christians, you should know that most evangelical Protestants in Europe also accept evolution. They have no trouble believing that perhaps God simply *used* evolution as a mechanism for creating life. They look at Bible verses like, "If your right hand causes you to sin, cut it off," and they say, "Well, of course that doesn't mean we should *literally* cut our hands off!" They look at Genesis and say something similar. They don't need everything to be absolutely literal. They're not American Fundies. They're grownups.

Or perhaps I've misread your motivations. Maybe you're sending me a final call for help, a plea for salvation from the grasps of The Saved. One last shot at truth, before you exit the world of the rational people.

Nah. Not likely. Because I saw the latest newspaper article.

It's amazing, you know. This year you've gotten more press coverage than any public-school teacher in the country, and when people ask me about you, I sound like the old Will Rogers radio program. "I only know what I read in the papers."

Dr. Kairns showed me the article, actually. It was this morning, during a meeting in his office, right after he told me that he'd be recommending me for tenure next year, as long as I keep up the good work. "Controversial Bio Teach Suspended!" said the headline. "Uses Creationist Textbook for Class," the subhead explained helpfully.

"Eh, this must be embarrassing for you," Kairns said. "But don't worry. This time around, they don't even mention he has a cousin." A joke! A wonderful rarity from Kairns.

"I never talk to him anymore," I told him.

"We've all got some strange rangers in our family trees," he reassured me. "Remind me to tell you some day about my aunt the clairvoyant."

And off I went to teach my Micro II course, awash in the renewed hopes of a good review to the tenure committee.

I will not respond to your questions and challenges about science, Mikey. You know why? Because your new friends will have answers to everything I say. They'll always have the last word, since they're now part of your life, and since I'm not. Instead, I'll leave your challenges and questions unanswered. They'll always hang there in your mind. You'll always wonder what I would have said, and wonder whether there's some greater truth you've missed. Some way of life that rejoices in finding more and more questions, rather than a life spent sitting contentedly atop an ancient pile of pre-made answers.

No more science. Instead, I'll talk to you about religion. Your religion, and the religion of your new friends.

How's church? Have you been baptized yet? I hope so, for your sake, so that the Fundie Pentecostals will fully embrace you as one of their own. Be sure to adopt all the important philosophies of Christianity as soon as possible: an opposition to abortion, a hatred of evolution, a loathing of homosexuals, all those things Jesus never mentioned, but which are the driving force of today's best and brightest faiths. Speak in tongues! Do it often! It's the surest way of keeping yourself from saying anything intelligible to the real world. Frankly, I'd prefer that.

Here's some news you might find interesting. I've been reading the Bible. Now, don't get all excited and hopeful that I'm a candidate for your new club. I came close to self-loathing and despair, but it was never really the sort of downer that could push me into fantasies of repentance. As a matter of fact, I haven't read a lot of the Bible yet . . . I'm sure the Old Testament has many beautiful passages, but the first one I opened to was Deuteronomy chapter 23, which commanded me to always carry a shovel so that I can bury the results of bowel movements I have outdoors.

Maybe I'll try a different Old Testament book later on, but I switched to the one writer I thought I might like, St. Paul. I think I mentioned before that I admired what he had to say about glossolalia . . . you know, how only babbling fools thought it was an important part of faith?

He was an interesting guy. You should read him some time. I mean all of him, not just the parts your Pente-fundie-costals point you to, the parts that back up their beliefs. St. Paul's not always consistent (oh, heavens, did I just say that? Blasphemy!), but he has some real kickers in his epistles.

I'm changing my mind about a couple of things. For example: where did I pick up that Paul was a woman hater? Sure, some of the things he said are harsh on the ears of this post-feminist age, but, man! Given his age and time, he was pretty impressive. Consider that women had almost *no* rights in Paul's culture, less freedom than even the Roman and Greek cultures allowed their ladies (which wasn't much). So when Paul tosses out the line, "Women who prophesy in the assembly should keep their heads covered," he's delivering more than a rule about headdress. Behind his words is the subtle, revolutionary pronouncement: "Hey, women are allowed to be prophets, and they can talk in the church." Compare that to the number of women allowed to talk in the first-century synagogues Paul was accustomed to, and you can see what I mean about radical.

And slavery? Paul's culture didn't consider slavery a bad thing (although I suppose the slaves felt differently about that). The institution of slavery was a critical economic and social force of the world in those days, and offered a lot more cross-cultural, equal-opportunity forced employment than the blacks-only system of the early U.S. I haven't read everything Paul wrote yet, so I can't say he *never* spoke directly against slavery, but I did read his short epistle to a guy named Philemon . . . and, wow, does he turn on the psychological warfare, forcing Philemon to reconsider out-and-out ownership of another human being . . . again, startlingly radical for the day and age. He walks the edge. He's always right on the brink of turning the world upside down.

Your church could learn a lot from him. Have they read all his stuff yet? I heartily recommend it. They might consider lingering on the line, "If I speak with the tongues of men, or even of angels, but do not have love, I am just a noisy gong, a clanging cymbal."

You know, "love." The kind your friends employed when they tricked their kids into becoming foot soldiers in the war against you, and the profound love that went into destroying my fly lab and trying to destroy my career. That's the sort of love St. Paul would have admired. The real proactive kind.

Honestly, though, I don't think St. Paul and I would have seen eye-to-eye on most things, especially that whole bit about repentance. I guess I respect it as a tactic for expanding his organization; what better way to get people to turn their lives over to you, than by making them loathe and reject everything they've been previously? It's kind of like what you're going through these days . . . suspended from your job, being forced to renounce the only family you have left, turning away from science, wholesale. A completely new life. Born again in every possible way!

But they're still keeping their eyes on you. You're not completely there yet, despite any degrees of illusion you might have about your place in their little circle. How do I know that? The tone of the letter you sent me. The desperate plea, wanting me to fire the last volley that sets you free from rationality. Over and over again, you used the phrase, "And how would you answer *that?*" At first I thought it was a rhetorical device. The eighth time I read it, I knew that you really were asking, even if only subconsciously.

Maybe I was wrong. If you'd really repented and surrendered your life to these people, my opinion would mean nothing to you. Maybe you're still the same Mikey, doing things half-assed. Not really going all the way in science, and stopping short before reaching your full potential. Not really going all the way in religion, and stopping short of full repentance, full surrender. I won't go as far as your father would . . . calling you a "bloody half-wit" . . . but your lack of commitment certainly brings those terms to mind.

I only want what's best for you, Mikey. Even now, when you're so closely tied with my enemies. If true repentance is really your goal, then my hope for you is that you'll put your entire heart into it. Really confess your sins, really reject your old ways, really start your life anew. I don't want to be embarrassed about being related to you. I want, at the very least, to be proud, and to be able to say, "Mikey knows what he believes, and he embraces it to its fullest. I may not agree with him, but I admire his conviction."

To help you out on that path, I have mailed a letter to Giselle. In it, I detailed our incestuous relationship, told her many of the graphic details, and urged her to question you fully on it, that you might find real repentance through her help. Since your new friends are true Christians, I'm sure she'll love you even more, now that she knows.

By my guess, the letter arrived in today's mail. Hey, maybe you should tell her to get email. It really is a lot easier, you know.

Your affectionate cousin,
Doctor Lillian

—25—

Greetings to my kind, the No-Flesh Asarkos,

I was given the answer to a question I did not ask; and what I had not been seeking, I found.

That night, with Sarkate eyes, I saw one of Our Enemies.

At Martha's house, both Luke and I knocked, but the door was not opened. I knew I had again been fooled, once more eluded by a Sarkate who had knowledge of my kinsmen, knowledge I required. The dwelling was deserted.

"You will not find anyone within," Blastus's voice called from the shadows to our left, a few steps north along Cyranos Street. "I have tracked them to the city's southern walls, in the district of temples, but I could not keep up to follow them further and determine where they hide."

"Well done, nonetheless, my friend," I said, approaching him. "Lead us to where you lost track of them."

Luke pushed past me. He took hold of Blastus and directed him closer to the nearest burning street lamp. "I thought as much," Luke said, sounding angry. "The very idea that you might not be able to keep up with any living soul!" Luke had pushed aside the outer mantle Blastus wore as a night coat, and revealed a gaping sword wound in our Roman friend's side. The injury did not look fresh; much of the blood had seeped and dried into the cloth of his inner tunic. "It makes no matter to me that the two of you keep secrets. But some secrets must be shared with your physician!"

"I knew nothing of this!" I insisted, and then realized that Luke's anger was of a more general nature and not entirely focused on this single incident.

"You have been running around with this injury most of the day!" Luke tore away large sections of the inner garment, revealing all of the wound. The laceration was as long as my forearm, and looked very deep.

"Most of two days," Blastus said. "They came upon me yesterday. I am sorry. It seems that word of my treasonous status has at last reached Antioch."

"I have no medicines with me," Luke muttered. "I need wine, a strong wine to burn corruption from the wound."

"A Roman soldier did this to you?" I could not conceive of such a thing, knowing the utter loyalty Blastus gave to the soldiery and to Rome.

"Five tried, one succeeded," Blastus confirmed. "I could not harm them. I could no more put steel into a brother in Roman uniform than I could kill either of you, the last friends I have to love in this damned world."

The concern on Luke's face deepened. "This is bad. He is losing his mind and claiming he loves us." Luke pressed the back of his hand against the side of Blastus's face. "Fever. The corruption has entered his blood."

Blastus pushed his hand away. "My mind is intact. Savor the admission of friendship, little Greek, because I will not be repeating it."

"Sit down, sit on the stones," Luke said gently.

Instead, Blastus turned and dashed from us, headed toward the darkness of the alley nearby.

—

In the alley between the house of Martha and a shop selling metalwares, Blastus secured the arms of Thomas the Apostle in what must have been a rather uncomfortable grip. The rough hold probably did not matter to

Thomas as much as the blade of Blastus's sword mattered, the length of which was firmly positioned at Thomas's neck. "You will tell Paul of Tarsus what he demands to know."

Luke and I entered the alley, surprised at the catch Blastus had made, and surprised that we the spy-ers had been spied upon.

"Paul," Thomas pleaded, "would you truly threaten me, a friend of your people and a brother in The Way of the Risen Christ?"

When I said nothing in reply, and simply glared my anger at him, Luke stepped forward to fill the silence. "Thomas," he said, "I would tell him what he wants to know, and in a most hurried manner at that. Yours is not the only life in peril tonight."

Blastus glared, his face making it clear that Luke should by no means reveal that Thomas was held captive by a man of disappearing strength.

"Thomas the Doubter, Apostle of Christ, I would see the woman Esther, wife of Judah." My words were steady, and my tone was cold. "You will make that possible, else you yourself will never again see or hear or taste anything upon this Earth."

"That is why I came!" Thomas the Apostle pleaded. "I was here to bring you to Esther, and to your kinsmen!"

"Hiding in shadows is not so immediate a way to approach us," I said. "Were you waiting for anything in particular, or simply eavesdropping in curiosity?" Luke said nothing during this exchange; his eyes stayed on Blastus, worrying, studying the Roman's condition.

"Not all are invited to come." Thomas summoned as much dignity as one could expect from a man with a sword at his neck. "Some mysteries must stay mysteries."

"My friends come with me," I said, "and you are in no position to grant selective invitations."

Certainly I was aware of the commotion coming from the south end of Cyranos Street, but I was too furious with Thomas to allow it to distract me. What did distract me was the change in Blastus's face, a change from pained, focused determination, to a complete loosening of his facial muscles, sad but peaceful resignation. Had I not noticed that, I would have noticed the lowering of his sword from the doubting Apostle's neck.

"You summoned the governor's guards," Blastus said to Thomas.

"Some mysteries must remain mysteries," Thomas repeated.

I looked up the street. They made their presence plain by the torches they carried. There were eight guards in all.

"What fools," Blastus said without emotion. "Boisterous, torches signaling their presence, approaching as a tight group; all of it folly. Had I the will or the strength, I could circle, stalk from the darkness, and have half of them down before the other half knew I was upon them."

Thomas straightened his robe, smoothing the balling and wrinkles left by Blastus's grip. "This alley empties to a small pathway left for the street's sewage channel. Come, Paul of Tarsus, and bring your Gentile physician. The balm he uses to cure the eye scales is of great interest to your kinsmen."

"I will not leave Blastus to die!"

Thomas snorted. "They do not kill their own without a trial. Come, let us leave the Romans to their own affairs."

"Paul, he is already dead," Luke said quietly. "And he knows it. The corruption is everywhere in his blood."

Blastus made no attempt to disagree. "Paul of Tarsus, I would have you know that our new emperor will be announced at first light tomorrow. One day if you should find yourself in Rome, argue my case and my honor before Claudius Caesar."

"You will not die," I insisted. "I know nothing of this blood corruption claimed by Luke. I do know Roman law, and I will stand beside you as a citizen and witness to ensure these guards follow it to the letter and leave you unharmed!"

Blastus lifted his sword anew. To his credit, he did not allow the strain of the action to show in his face. "They will have no choice in the matter of engaging me. You must promise to go to Rome. Claudius is an addled fool, but even your weak preaching and the Greek's dull rhetoric are better representation than none at all. You will persuade him. Now go."

He left, then. He walked into the street, his sword before him, and he proceeded south toward his kinsmen, his enemies.

—

There are fevers and ailments and plagues, Luke tells me, brought on not by the imbalance of a body's humors, but by other sources he cannot yet name. He speculates that unseen powers can enter a body, causing illness from the outside as surely as a blade might pierce one through and bring death in that manner. He further speculates, in contrast to his first speculations, that the invading illness is not carried by forces at all, but by physical matter too small to be seen by the eyes, smaller even than the sand mites one must struggle to observe. Some Greek philosophers, his kinsmen, hold to the idea of "atoms," small and indivisible units of matter, of which are constituted all things that can be seen. Luke thinks there may be poison atoms, invaders that creep into open wounds and bring corruption to the body that is sometimes more dangerous than the wound itself. Pouring strong wine in the wound sometimes helps, and sometimes does not. Luke thinks that he can make some of the poison atoms drunk and unable to perform their deadly tasks. Others among the poison atoms do not respond to the wine, much as some men can take their drinks for hours on end but still show no effect. He continues to refine this theory, even to this day.

Blastus died, and I now believe he would have died regardless. I did not think so that night. I stopped our escape five house-rows down from the house of Martha of Bethany, turning up the first accessible alley we encountered. I looked carefully around the corner, onto Cyranos Street. Blastus was taking the last of his blows from the palace guardsmen. Two of the swords had come free from their wielders' grips, and stayed embedded in my friend. One sword grip protruded from behind, evidence that a coward among them had stabbed Blastus in the back. Blastus's sword slashed the air; to the end, he was careful not to strike a single one of his uniformed comrades.

He fell without valiant declaration, noble last words, or curses against Rome.

"What do you see?" the voice of Thomas asked from behind me.

"My friend, and the longtime colleague of Saul, lying dead in the street."

"Is that what you see?" Thomas whispered. "Then he is not dead, he is only asleep."

I looked harder. Several of the guardsmen's torches had been dropped in the battle they imagined to be real, so it was difficult to make out details. But then I needed no torches to see. A different light, startlingly red, detached from the body of Blastus and rose to hover above it. Its intensity took my breath from me; it lighted the street from south to north, bringing every detail into reddish relief.

Thomas heard my gasp. "Now," he said, "he is dead."

The soldiers did not seem to notice the light. "Do you see it?" I asked Thomas.

"No, but it has been described to me." His sigh was decidedly profound.

I knew then that I saw not with Sarkate eyes, but with the part of me that was truly me, along the receptor frequencies I adopt for capturing and processing unsolicited input. The light was not a physical occurrence; it was a manifestation of my immaterial cosmos. With Asarkos capabilities and Sarkate eyes of flesh, I could see what could not be seen by Thomas, by the soldiers, by Luke.

The redness deepened and darkened. "The frequency is shifting," I said. And then I understood why the Sarkate, beings of matter, could have sentience, despite the protestations of our best Asarkos thinkers. It was because the Sarkate are not only flesh; within them, they carry what we would call waves, for need of better words. Primitive, sentient waves.

The red had turned nearly to black as the length of Blastus's wave increased. Saul's Sarkate eyes were losing track of the manifestation, unskilled at interpreting the ranges of resonating data I still collected. Soon, I too was losing the ability to perceive. But the last burst of data I could access made a very clear impression on me.

"I know that pattern. I recognize the intermix of frequencies and the rate of shift!"

Thomas was pulling me back from the alley's opening, touching his lips to signal me to lower my voice.

"The Sarkate wave essence shifts to lower frequencies," I said. "Man's soul. Men are Our Enemies!"

Luke had not ventured up the alley with Thomas. We rejoined him at the rear.

"They destroy us, Luke," I said, not being careful with my words. "They shift to nullify our frequencies, and we are eradicated from the cosmos. That is why there were so many around this world! It is the starting point, and they congregate about it. Men are Our Enemies!"

Luke said nothing, which was probably for the best at that time. My understanding had been shaken, and I could no longer think of things in the way I had been thinking them.

Thomas spoke sharply to me. The Apostle Thomas . . . a Sarkate for whom I had wished nothing but retribution over the past several days. But anger that strong cannot be maintained, not when one has discovered that the universe, really, is not just as one has described it to oneself. No loves or hatreds stand before a moment such as that.

"We must go *now*," Thomas insisted. "Esther has fallen ill again, and the time is short before she leaves us."

"Esther?" I said. "But she has become better now. Esther has stopped being dead."

It is the endless rhythm of the Sarkate: no life is permanent, and the change of death must come. But it did not seem fair. We had cheated death. It did not seem right for its time to come again to Esther, at least not so soon.

"We must go now," Thomas repeated. And so we did, immediately, on that night when there was too much death and dying.

Yours from among the Sarkate,

Paul of Tarsus

—26—

SENT BY: Lillian.Uberland@rsi.edu
RECEIVED BY: MNA@sellenville.edu

Cousin,

My god, I didn't know. What were you thinking? I never, never, never, never would have sent that letter to Giselle if you'd been straightforward with me. Jesus, Jesus, what are we going to do?

Dr. Kairns is a smart man. He knows a lot of people. He must know some lawyers, somebody who can make this go away. But I'm terrified to say anything to him. How can I say anything to anyone after this? It's my fault, oh my sweet Michael. I have never learned to keep my mouth shut!

You should have told me that the suspension for teaching Creationism in class was only the school district's cover story. Was I supposed to *guess* that you were being investigated for having an affair with Mousy Girl? Are charges of statutory rape the sort of thing I'm just supposed to *pick up* from a frantic, angry string of questions about evolution and science? Christ almighty, Michael, why did you stop trusting me? Why the hell did you stop confiding in me?

That mother of hers, Giselle, that bitch. I *handed* her what she needed. That letter will turn you into a monster in front of any jury on the face of the Earth. Oh my god, I gave her the final nail for the coffin they were building for you. You know she isn't doing this alone. This came from that entire church. I told you, I told you long ago that they were dangerous, and that if you became an "issue," they would turn into a pack of dogs, gang up with power no one could imagine. Christians? These people aren't Christians, they're the force of evil hiding under that title. This lie, from those monsters! And I was wrong about the kids, too. They've already turned the children evil, especially if Mousy Girl is talked into taking the stand and telling those lies to a court. Baal-zebub, they called me? *They're* Baal-zebub! Oh my god, Michael, these people are more wicked than I could dream. They aren't Fundies or Pentecostals, not really. I'm willing to say Fundies are idiots and power-hungry and blissfully free of the burden of rationality, but this evil, this utter wickedness? No. Something's wrong. This enemy isn't the enemy I thought it was. This is horrible.

It hasn't made the papers. If what you tell me is everything there is so far, they're still investigating. The police know, of course, but no charges are filed, that would have hit the media for sure. Why the hell haven't you gotten a lawyer? I'll talk to Kairns. He's smart. He reminds me of your father, he's that smart, he'll tell me what to do, where to find the best lawyer in the world.

Oh my god, Michael. You needed me to be unselfish, and all I've been is obstinate and self-righteous. I'm sorry, I'm sorry. What are we going to do?

Come to me. I can't stand only writing to you or talking to your answering machine. Come to me as soon as you read this. I can't bear to think of you, all alone. I can't bear to be alone. We'll stop them. There's only us, just like always, and we'll stop this somehow if only we have each other.

I love you.

I need to see you.

I have to fight this with you.

I need to hear you say, just once, that it really isn't true. Then we'll fight them.

Your cousin,
Doctor Lillian

—27—

Greetings to my kind, the No-Flesh Asarkos,

We arrived at an abandoned temple. Upon the grounds in front of it stood an altar so small that it did not come as high as my waist. Its solemn dedication read: "To The Unknown Gods." Despite hundreds of deities honored throughout Antioch, it seems the citizens took no chance at offending heaven, honoring even gods they might have missed.

In an upper room of that temple to the unknown gods, I met The Ten Who Were Missing. You know their names well, my dear Asarkos brethren; or, if you do not, and if you are newly arrived to this planet of our salvation, they are names that you will know soon enough.

Philemon and his wife Apphia of Colossae; Theophilus and Timothy, two young men who clung to one another as if lovers; Silas who would one day preach throughout the world with me, and Barnabas who is likewise a dear fellow laborer; Mary of Bethany and her brother Lazarus, both siblings of Martha, and Lazarus being the same man whom we are told was raised from death by the Sarkate Jesus; and Titus and Sylvanus of Antioch, Gentiles from the very city in which I was now meeting The Ten.

Of course I did not know their names upon entering the room. But I did know in an instant that these were my kinsmen, the missing ones for whom I had traveled so very, very far.

They were silent when I entered. Mary of Bethany greeted me first, giving a kiss to my right cheek, then a kiss to my left. Barnabas was next, a kiss and a kiss, followed by a vigorous embrace. The remaining eight did not approach me physically; instead they reached out in the Asarkos way, flooding me with rapid data, silent greetings and detailed information of each of their lives, of how they had come to inhabit the bodies of the Sarkate, and introductions to the Sarkate spirits, still present in all of them and each woven without seam into the personalities of their Asarkos companions. Ten bodies, twenty sentient beings, a flood of experience I could follow with my mind, but which caused the brain of Saul to dizzy, and caused the body of Saul to sink gently to one knee.

"I have been in the city for days," I managed. "You might have been more timely in making my acquaintance."

I saw it all, every answer at once: the grave of Lazarus at Bethany, and the profound despair of Mary, who had given up hope upon the death of her brother. Mary's surrender to the first of the arriving Asarkos, and the miraculous ability of Jesus to place a second within the body of Lazarus . . . a body not yet dead, but only sleeping. The months they spent waiting for the scales upon their eyes to finally loosen and drop free. Then two years later, the day of feasting called Pentecost by the Jews, at which the Apostles, themselves but Sarkate, boldly proclaimed their understanding of the Risen Christ, and the large crowd in Jerusalem to which they preached. Mary and Lazarus standing with the Apostles that day, urging them, encouraging the effort. The power of the Apostles' message, striking to despair and repentance so many throughout the crowd; the Sarkate of the mob, many driven to that moment of which Thomas spoke, the moment of despairing surrender when life and death were both the same, and no hope remained. The arrival of the final eight of ten, who freely selected from among dozens in the crowd, inhabiting and scaling the eyes of eight additional bodies. And in the years that passed, the development of their craft: the conversion of Sarkate, and the guidance of arriving Asarkos waves into new homes of flesh.

There, on one knee in that upper room, I laughed for joy. "You were never within the Apostles!" I cried. "You were among them, but never within!"

Thomas helped me to my feet. "And you!" I said. "You could not accept what the other Apostles believed had happened to the crowd, to these people, my brethren. You thought there was more to be known. You were . . . a fanciful supposer among the Sarkate!"

"And I was right," he said calmly. "For which the Apostles have rewarded me the name Thomas the Doubter, a title I seem unable to escape." With a more serious tone, he told me, "The Apostles do not know. I think, perhaps, they can never know."

"Then I should like to meet them," Luke said, addressing us for the first time since we entered the building, "for I would feel at home in their knowledge-free company."

I should have realized that Luke was the sole inhabitant of the room who did not understand what was taking place. "There is a scroll," I said to him. "When we return to the home of Trophimos, you must read it. It documents all my thoughts since I first became Paul of Tarsus, right to the day before we entered Antioch. You will understand much more once you read it."

"I am touched by your new desire for candor, dear old friend of Tarsus." I was confused by the harsh quality of his voice. "But my only aim now is to see to the needs of a dying woman."

"Is she here as Thomas promised?" I asked them.

Mary of Bethany did not answer me, but instead addressed Luke. "Friend of my kinsman, your motives are strong and appreciated, but we are well past the hours in which your ministrations could have aided her."

"She is dead?" I asked, trying not to let The Ten see how deeply felt my question was.

In answer, Martha of Bethany, the human-only sister of Mary and Lazarus, emerged from the room adjoined to the main upper level. "She can feel him here," Martha said. "She would see Paul of Tarsus now. There is not much time."

She said it in the Ugaritic tongue, but all present understood, including James, I think. As Luke moved past her, into the room, he paused long enough to mutter, "One day I would learn from you how you came to speak that language."

"My brother and sister taught me," she said. "It is the language of angels."

Lazarus stopped me before I followed Luke in. "Forgive us. Due to Esther's arrival, we did not come for you immediately. You came here as we did, but her coming was different. She came at our summons. We have learned to reach out to our kind."

I was stunned; I was conflicted. I wanted to learn which combination of frequencies could be used to summon our kind. But more than that, I longed to see Esther again.

—

I am still ashamed at my revulsion to the wasted, bruised, decaying body of Esther, and to the odor of fleshy rot that hung thick in the air. Judah sat in the far corner of the smaller room, away from the matting upon which Esther lay. "Good," he said. "You have found us. Now you can make her well again, if that pleases you." They were words of hope, spoken without any evidence of hopefulness.

I had halted in my steps when the odors overtook me, so it embarrassed me to see Luke pay them no heed. He went directly to Esther and removed the blankets that covered her. Even in the dark I could see that her skin was a leprous mess, but he first looked at her eyes. I do not know why; I am no physician.

"Paul of Tarsus." Her voice was a distant whisper. It did not seem possible she could be conscious. It did not seem she should be alive.

"I would have another lamp in here," Luke muttered. I made no move to fetch one. Even I could weigh the matter and come to a verdict. I looked to Judah, who did not look back. I do not think he could even see the world, this world, his and mine.

"How long will she live?" I asked Luke.

"Until yesterday," he said with consternation, "or perhaps the day before."

"Paul of Tarsus, come here now." I could sense the Asarkos within her. I knew that was who spoke to me; I recognized the resonations, but of course had no name by which to address my kinsman.

I summoned strength to withstand my revulsion and approached the bed matting. I breathed shallowly, but it helped little. "My own eyes have beheld Lazarus of Bethany, long ago risen from the dead, with no ill effects. Why is this happening to her?"

Luke did not answer. He left Esther's side and moved to Judah. The Damascan Jew paid no heed to Luke's examination.

A hand grabbed mine, and a shiver ran through me. "Let him tend the living," Esther's voice bade me.

"I cannot see her like this," I said, addressing my kinsman within her. "How could this befall her?"

"It was already here." Each word she spoke came with inhuman effort. Asarkos effort, I suppose. "This illness could not be overcome. I fought it with her. But the flesh was too weak."

"I told you," Luke said. I thought he had not been listening. "Invisible corruptions invade the body. Does this surprise you, of all people, yourself an invader?"

"But Lazarus—"

"—must have died of something else!" His was the fury of a man beaten but railing defiance against the defeat. "Something that *new* strength could cure. Something . . . not like this, with her. I do not have any answers! But I know cruelty when I see it. Make your kinsman let her go." Luke sat on the floor beside the impassive Judah, all anger emptied from him at once. "It is torture. Your people must let her go."

Her hand, encrusted with dried pus and slippery with new secretions, squeezed mine gently. "The physician is wrong. I said we should die. I would not torture. She begged us to stay. She begged to see you."

I did not take my eyes from hers. They seemed the only bits of her still living. "Shall I let her speak with Saul?" I asked. I believe my voice trembled. I believe I have never felt such strong feelings, not before then, not since.

"She knows no Saul. Esther would speak with *you*, kinsman."

I saw no change, but I knew it was Esther who spoke next.

"Spirit from above, did you truly love me? Or did I imagine?"

"My flesh felt great passion," I said. I was crying now, and I remembered the wailing and lamentations of Judah at Esther's first death. I would not do that, but I understood the need. "Yes. There was love. The thought of you, just the thought, gave me strength. In this world, I was a foreigner in a foreign land. But striving to find you, I could bear all things, retain all faith and hope, endure all things. What I felt for you knew no boundaries."

She released my hand. "Then I was right. You loved me, just as I loved you."

Esther receded, my kinsman emerged. "That is what she wished to say. Tell The Ten that now I can die. They worry. None has yet died within the flesh, and they long to know what happens."

"Let them stay outside." I made no effort to hide my tears. "I will impart to them any critical data."

"Watch carefully," the waning whisper bade me. "I wish to test some thoughts I have."

It was true Asarkos motivation, the desire for more input, the need to know more even at the brink of oblivion. That, I believe, is why death cannot stand against us, or finally conquer our flesh-free sentient drive. By knowing more, we bring more order to the cosmos, even if only within our understanding of what reality is. The universe stretches, cools, and slowly brings toward death all energy and matter within it. But *We Are*, and nothing can change that. We always will have been, even after the End of All.

Esther died.

I felt a frequency, an emanation that was shifting its wavelength, oscillating short to long, to shorter again, to longer still. A beckoning, a summons? It caught me by surprise, and I did not analyze the input quickly enough. Distraction came fast, for another presence filled the room. A new Asarkos—not myself, not the kinsman of late within Esther, but a third, arriving along the path of the summons.

Esther's Asarkos called out to our kind.

None of this could be perceived by Luke, of course, and he later told me he thought I had gone mad with grief, given the way my head turned and swiveled, desperately trying to look in all directions at once. My attention was pulled from the invisible to the visible; Judah stood, his hands shaking and his eyes wide with wonder. "Yes," he said. Then again he said, "Yes."

Luke tried to steady our friend the Jew, but I placed a staying hand upon the physician's shoulder, drawing him back.

For a space of ten heartbeats, all quieted. Nothing remained in that room, nothing but a Greek, a wayward Pharisee, and me, the Pharisee's uninvited inhabitant. Judah's flesh stood there, for several moments empty of sentience. Then all about him came the light, and the winds, and manifestations that you, my readers, now know so well from my descriptions of the road to Damascus and Esther's resurrection in the desert. You have those data, so I see no need to repeat them.

Here, though, came the variation that made the data far more interesting.

Judah walked to me when the light was gone. His hands reached out and touched my arms, for he could not see; the rapid growth of scales already had blocked his eyes.

"It has been eons, my love," Judah said to me. In an instant I knew that it was Esther speaking. Also present was her Asarkos companion. I could not detect the essence that once was Judah.

"It has only been a few moments," I said.

"For you," said Esther.

"I thought you would transform into one of Our Enemies," I said. "That is what happened to Blastus."

"So long ago," she agreed. Within me, I felt stirrings from Saul of Tarsus; he was agitated, disconcerted by communing with the essence of Esther while hearing the voice and seeing the form of Judah. I felt none of that.

Judah-Who-Is-Esther greeted me in the manner of the brethren, a kiss and a kiss. "How tempted I was to stay!" she said. "Judah remained, but I could not. So long ago you told me that love knows no boundaries, and I have returned to show you it is true."

"We said that just a few moments ago," I claimed.

Luke separated us and touched a finger to one of the eye scales. He prodded where the leathery scab joined healthy flesh. "While you two speak your meaningless words, I would like to continue being a physician. Could we please send someone to Trophimos's home to fetch my damned medicines?"

I was glad the scales remained for now. Elsewise, Judah's eyes would behold the dead body of Esther behind me; she had no need to see what had become of her, even if, as she now claimed, the moment of her death was eons past.

"Invite The Ten inside the room," Esther said. "We have much to show you. For we have been to the unbounded Now of eternity, and we know the secret path that leads there."

I hastened to gather The Ten. Luke left to get his medicines. He was exasperated with the lot of us.

Yours from among the Sarkate,
Paul of Tarsus

—28—

Cousin,

It feels very strange to be writing an actual snail-mail letter to you, rather than an email. I know, I know, you type a regular letter on a computer, just like you type an email. But the thought of having to print it, fold it up, put it in an envelope, affix a stamp, address it to a prison . . . it all adds to the feeling of your being so far away from me, locked up and awaiting trial.

No bail! What, do they think you're some kind of mass murderer? I would have paid anything, gone three lifetimes into debt to get you out. I guess it was your youth; they considered you a flight risk, with no ties to the community and less than a year of residence there. Brother. Sellenville. Do I correctly recall telling you that town wasn't quite the sticks? I was wrong. It really is the sticks, at least in its heart, where it counts.

They take my deposition tomorrow. The court will term me a "hostile witness" at the request of the prosecution. I thought that would give you a chuckle, thinking that anyone might imagine *me* to be hostile.

Here's something to take your mind off life and reality and all these things that suck over the past few months. Remember my fruit flies, the ones with the scaled eyes? And how I had a dream that they were flying around my head, singing to me? I was sitting at home eating breakfast yesterday, and suddenly I remembered: I was playing the radio the day those larvae hatched, and I left it on as background noise. I mean, I left it on for weeks, maybe even throughout the entire life cycle of that batch of flies. I was the only one who used the fly lab last semester, and I stayed late so often that the background noise of the radio made me feel a little less alone.

So it strikes me: could that be the one variable I had overlooked? I'd tested for everything else, everything you could imagine, and if I still had my notebooks, I could prove that. So I called Kairns and ran the ridiculous radio idea by him. You know what? He laughed at me, and again said, "You are so obsessed, Lillian. It makes you a good scientist, but it also makes you a pain in my butt."

I wasn't in a laughing mood, and I tried to get him to consider the possibility of electromagnetic interference somehow affecting hatching *Drosophila*, causing a disturbances that made their eyes encrust. He wasn't buying it. He thinks I should go back to considering normal infection agents like bacteria or viruses, and the auto-immunal responses of fruit flies. You know, the kinds of things that make humans generate more blood cells, and that promote scarring and scabbing on the surface of human bodies.

I told him I'd looked into all that, and that it wouldn't hurt to spend some of my own free time investigating fruit flies and energy fields. And you know what? He laughed again, and said he'd see if anyone in the Physics Department would be interested in working with me on it. Just like that, I'm assigned a physics doctoral candidate, and I'm spending approved preliminary research time investigating that angle. Physics is amazing. I mean the stuff beyond the basic courses we took in college. There are areas of quantum speculation I didn't even dream were being seriously investigated: multi-dimensions, multi-universes, whole new realities that come in sizes too small to even think about. To make a long story short, I've decided that next semester I'm going to audit some advanced physics courses, maybe look into how likely it would be to one day get a second Ph.D. under my belt. Lumping biology with physics, all in one brain . . . Kairns says it would be very cheeky of me, but I think he suspects I could pull it off. In time, though, in time.

I talked to your lawyer again today. He tells me they've put you on a suicide watch. That startled me, but he said I haven't seen how you've been regressing over the past few weeks. He's worried. I'm sorry I haven't been out to see you. Things have been crazy. You know how it is.

Michael, I have to tell them the truth in the deposition tomorrow. I have no choice. I thought about claiming that I made up the whole incest thing to cause trouble for you and to gross out that bitch Giselle. I was willing to perjure myself. But your lawyer turned pale when I suggested that. I guess they have strict rules, and he was required to insist, pretty forcefully, that I not lie when under oath. If I had lied to him, too, I could have gotten away with it; but I guess he's required to keep me from perjury, now that he knows.

But the fact is, Michael, that I now believe I should tell them the truth anyway, regardless of how I feel.

All you had to tell me was that it hadn't happened. You just had to assure me that while chastely dating the mother, you weren't having an affair with the daughter. *Raping* her, Michael, because that's what statutory rape really is. It doesn't matter that she consented. She was under sixteen; she had no consent to give. It doesn't matter that she now says . . . still says . . . that she loves you. Under law, her love is meaningless. Maybe hundreds of years ago your relationship with her would have been "natural." Now it's just criminal, if it really happened.

You never denied it, Michael. I asked you directly, and you never said it was a lie.

All the evidence they'll squeeze out of me is circumstantial, but it doesn't paint a very good picture when you set it next to her testimony. They've even subpoenaed our old emails, Mikey, and early on you were very flattering in your descriptions of her. I'd erased all my old copies of the emails, but apparently they don't just disappear. Records are kept in archives. You learn something new every day, huh?

I hope you're not getting newspapers while you're in prison. You're a front-pager almost every day, and I'm afraid they're not saying very nice things about you. Do prisons let you read papers? Probably, because I know they have cable television in there. So I'm sure you've seen a lot of things already. I'm sorry. What you're going through is horrible, horrible.

That doesn't mean you should be thinking about suicide. You need to survive this, Michael. Don't make me lose you. While you live, there is still hope, always, forever.

Well, there's not much more to say, except that I'm going to have to tell them everything about us tomorrow, and that I'm sorry. I'm not sorry it happened; that memory I'll always cherish. But I'm sorry that the very thing I most cherish will be the thing that helps convict you.

Your affectionate cousin,
Doctor Lillian

—29—

Greetings to my kind, the No-Flesh Asarkos,

My penchant for writing epistles has infected Luke. He has compiled a long history of Jesus of Nazareth, written as a letter to our friend Theophilus, one of The Ten Who Were Missing. That project having been finished and delivered many months ago, he now begins an account of the Apostles, their acts and doings since the early days of this movement. Here in our prison cell, he looked up from the scroll he was researching, a copy of an epistle I had written to the Corinthians shortly after the death of Claudius Caesar. "You have told the church in Corinth that women must remain silent in the gathering of believers."

"I do recall telling them that," I said.

"But earlier in the scroll, you command that women who pray or prophesy in the assembly of believers must do so with their heads covered."

"You feel they should be allowed to do so unveiled?" I smiled, knowing what bothered him, but giving him the pleasure of pointing it out to me. It brings him great joy to bicker.

"That is not the issue! Either they remain silent, or they are allowed to prophesy. You cannot have it both ways!"

I pretended to be angry with him. "I certainly can. Who are you to argue with an Apostle of the Most High?" But I could not help myself, and allowed a smile to form upon my lips. "Such a contradiction will eventually be noticed, and I suspect it will lead to much contention. Where there is contention, there is a chance for despair. And where there is despair, there is a chance for salvation."

Luke closed the scroll, grumbling. "You could learn to be more subtle with your machinations," he said.

"Subtlety is not my goal. My goal is to save the lives of my kinsmen, and the precious spirits of yours."

It is still impossible for us to say where the brain-bound mind of a Sarkate ends, and where a Sarkate's wave-made essence begins. We do know that the thing many Sarkate speculators have called the "spirit" leaves the body soon after the time of physical death; we also know that the "spirit" retains no vestige of memory. Data storage and retention are physical functions of fleshy brains; data use and data communication are attributes of waves. Of spirits.

For millions of years, this planet called the Earth has been leaking Sarkate spirits into the cosmos. It should have been no issue for us: they cluster here, the orb is small, and the cosmos is quite large. But we stumbled upon them, and having found them, were devoured by them. And then they began to move outward from here, instinctively seeking us. But they know not what they do.

It was, you see, all quite unintentional; the spirits of the Sarkate have no personality, per se, but within them is the latent experience of a life spent collecting input through the flesh. Their old flesh had decayed; we, being waves quite capable of receiving, seeking, processing, and using information, triggered within those mindless spirits a quite natural response. They must have us. They must seek out the receptors of information. They must find.

It is an unfortunate byproduct of that instinct that we of the Asarkos race are eradicated when they find us.

Is there enmity, then? Is there blame? Sarkate spirits do not mean to behave as they do; indeed, they have no meaning at all, no intentions.

One may as well declare enmity with a self-swallowed star for naturally attracting to itself all the essence of the universe; one may as well declare war on a gust of wind.

I began this writing, this *journey*, with two problems: the problem of Our Enemies, and how any approach to them destroys us; and the problem of our universe, how in time its vast expansion will dissolve the essence of my Asarkos kinsmen. Now I end the journey with a single solution to both: salvation through the flesh of man.

If we meet man in the cosmos, we are doomed.

If we meet man in the flesh, we are saved. Not only us, but man as well.

Let me tell you what we learned from my dearest love, my Esther.

—

Through Esther's eyes, and through the memories of her Asarkos, I saw a state of existence I cannot begin to explain. I have considered many metaphors, both material and waveform, to try to communicate the data; none sufficed. But I can say that where Esther traveled after death was very small . . . a frequency that by our current understanding should not even exist. We Asarkos speak of our theory of Maximum Frequencies; this is smaller. Luke speaks of the Greek concept called "atoms"; those do not even compare. For as small as either of our races might imagine things to be, there are infinities between the smallest points of matter and the tightest crests of waves.

And I do mean infinities, as far as I can understand Esther's data. At such sizes, there is no matter and there are no waves, and what we perceive as differences between matter and energy disappear, and the true essence of things is revealed.

In the few moments of Sarkate time I stood in the upper room with Esther dead and Judah empty, those two and their Asarkos companions spent lifetimes in infinity. Esther and her Asarkos returned, claiming the one healthy body nearest their point of origin, the body of Judah. Both

Esther and my kinsman speak with frustration when they try to describe their experience.

"All possible data are accessed at once," says my kinsman, "and all manners of processing them become available."

"You know everything," says Esther, "and you keep learning."

Both I, Paul, and my Sarkate, Saul, complain that such contradictions do little to help.

Esther and her Asarkos laugh, and agree. What they lack in explanation, they make up for in joy.

———

Luke has reviewed my writings. He is begrudgingly satisfied with my epistles, except this latest I now write. He chides me for having given up trying to explain the essence and nature of infinity.

We have become irritable old men, but our affection for one another is genuine. He tells me he wants never to participate in my infinities and spirit worlds, and wishes he had never known any of the truths he has learned since the day I walked the road to Damascus. I, too, wish that, I suppose, for Luke now knows too much to be tricked into the life-surrendering despair that allows my kinsmen the opportunity to join with and befriend a Sarkate soul. He remains fully human. He has tasted of the Tree of Knowledge, and cannot be saved.

At least, not yet.

We sit in a Roman prison. That is nothing unusual for me. In the decades since Esther's first foray into infinity, I have known the insides of any number of prisons. So have the Apostles, and so have The Ten. It appears many are distressed by the kind of trouble we stir up in Sarkate cultures. It is important that the Apostles never learn what we are really doing. They are far more gifted than me and my kinsmen at driving the Sarkate into despair, the kind of despair we Asarkos require to continue the coming of my people and the salvation of both races. We of our kind have managed to convert hundreds; they, in their ignorance, have converted thousands. Should the Apostles learn the truth, neither of our peoples will ever be set free.

Nine thousand, three hundred and nine Asarkos kinsmen have entered into the flesh of the Sarkate, at my last count. That averages to fewer than one per day since Esther's second resurrection within the flesh of Judah. Three hundred fifty-six of our kinsmen have passed into infinity. Unlike Esther, not one has returned. Part of me is angry, because we need much more help up here. Another part of me understands. I have not seen infinity, have only heard about it in the words of Esther. Yet even I long for it, and think I would not return if Esther were still not here upon the Earth.

But our progress is not good enough. With such slow headway, it will take us thousands of years to save my race. To my kinsmen, that will make little difference; their perception of passing time would turn those millennia into a few decades of waiting. But the Sarkate die in droves; if I could save all of them, I would. There are just too many to reach.

—

At dusk the guards told us that Pricilla, daughter of Trophimos, had arrived with the evening meal. She was later than usual, and I had allowed myself to grow anxious. This would be my last chance to see her in this flesh.

She hurried to set down the bread and porridge she carried. As I have said many times, and now commit here to writing, she has grown into a comely woman, and draws my eyes whether she wears the drab drapings of a Jewess or the less demure raiment of a Greek citizen. Today she wore the latter, a sleeveless blue chiton, girt just below her breasts, so her embrace touched me fully and allowed me to feel her warmth and full contours. She kissed my right cheek, then my left, then lingered with a third kiss upon my lips.

"My dearest Esther," I said when our lips parted.

Luke clucked his tongue in disapproval. "I would leave you two to your privacy, but the guards might take issue with my wandering off."

"You are jealous in the face of true love," Esther scolded.

"Please believe," Luke said, "that I find this preferable to your kissing him from behind the hairy, weathered lips of Judah, may he rest in his eternal sleep."

Pricilla-Who-Is-Esther looked surprised. "He does not rest at all, but lives in infinity, in eternal joy!"

Luke waved an age-spotted hand at her. "It is just a Greek expression."

We lay upon our sides and ate in silence, quickly. Food did not keep long in the evening heat of a Roman summer, and flies accumulated quickly when food was left uncovered. Esther lay beside me throughout the meal.

"Today they executed Simon Peter," Pricilla said when I finished. I had sat up. Her head rested upon my lap. Had I been a younger man, that would have elicited a physical response. These days, only the spirit was willing.

Peter, executed. It was not unexpected.

"That means time is short for Paul of Tarsus," she said.

"Tomorrow," I acknowledged. "I have been told as much by the guards. I look forward to meeting Nero. I would give this Caesar the opportunity to accept the Risen Christ as his savior. And more important, I would tell him that old story of the loyal servant of Rome, the man named Blastus. I will confess how I dishonored Blastus those many years ago, and how I myself started the riots of Damascus for which the nobleman was blamed."

Luke set down his bowl of wine. "Confessing responsibility for the unjust death of a Roman nobleman will not win you Caesar's favor."

"Nero can only kill me once. All that remains of Blastus is his name. Rome will remember that name as honorable, if that is the last thing I do."

Unwilling to discuss the inevitable, Luke stood from his meal. He walked to the back of the room that served as our cell, and there he paced, frowning. I watched above him, using the sight of the Asarkos; one of our kinsman hovered over him, unseen, and eternally patient. It was Esther's idea, a gift to me I think, because she knows how well I cherish the Sarkate Luke. I will not suffer him to share Blastus's fate, the eternal loss of personality without chance for infinity. The Asarkos summoned by Esther will wait, never leaving Luke, and joining with him in his last seconds, whether Luke's end comes through accident, or in the final surrender of old age's despair. It is a luxury, I know, considering how slowly the news of salvation spreads among the Asarkos, and how few of us have come, still, to work among the Sarkate.

Luke knows nothing of his unseen companion. It is the only bit of knowledge I keep from him.

"This time tomorrow, you will see infinity," Pricilla said.

"And moments later, I will return," I assured her.

"Many have not."

"That is their choice. I, for my part, have much work left to do here. And much love to support me as I do that work." I kissed her forehead tenderly. "We shall save our race, and bring the perfect knowledge of infinity to as many as we can."

"Perfect knowledge?" Luke snorted, and he walked back to the floor matting upon which our meal was set. "You claim your infinity holds perfect knowledge? The questions that remain! Tell me, please, how it is that the spirits of your kinsmen can merge so seamlessly with the souls of my people. Tell me why that merging opens the door to infinity, while, separate, the two races cannot attain it. Tell me why infinity is small, and not big." Luke sat back at his place; he waved his hand to disperse the flies that had congregated in the few moments he had walked away. "And tell me this, if you can tell me nothing else: who was Jesus of Nazareth?"

I set a hand upon Pricilla's cheek, caressing it. This was the question, the one that obsessed him. The day he first asked it, he added the study of histories to his studies of medicine.

"Was he an Asarkos?" Luke demanded.

"Mary and Lazarus of Bethany say he was not."

"Was he human?"

"No," I conceded, as I always conceded in this endless argument. "Not if the stories of his resurrection are true."

"Does he walk the Earth today? You, Esther-Pricilla-Judah, you who have twice been to infinity: did you happen to see him there in your travels? Ask him questions about who he might be, or why he started this strange adventure upon my world?"

"No," Pricilla said, smiling at our friend from her place on my lap. "For the millionth time, I do not know."

"There, then," Luke said, well enough satisfied with himself to finish his meal. "Perfect knowledge, you say. Ha. Perfect knowledge."

When all food was gone, the flies that had swarmed about it departed. It grew dark, and the guards came to release Pricilla. I longed for her to remain, wanting to hold her in my arms throughout the evening before my death. That was not permitted, of course, not even by the libertine Romans.

I gave her a scroll, an epistle to our brother Timothy that I completed yesterday. She stands now at the door, waiting for me to finish this. The Roman guards do not object. They are impressed with my courage in the face of death, unaware that I feel neither courage nor cowardice in these moments. They know this is their last night of duty overseeing me. They grant the gift of patience to a tired, old man whom they presume to be brave.

How surprised they would be to know that after my execution, I will be back among them in no time.

Yours from among the Sarkate,
Paul of Tarsus

—30—

SENT BY: Lillian.Uberland@rsi.edu
RECEIVED BY: MNA@sellenville.edu

To You Who Are My Cousin, My Kinsman, And My Friend,

A kiss upon your left cheek, and a kiss upon your right, as is the custom of those who follow The Way.

Well, I am quite pleased to have this over with, and again to have you back among those who strive to save mankind. Has your time in infinity been fruitful? Have you made any progress tracking down the elusive non-human, non-Sarkate named Jesus the Christ? And most especially, have you missed my endless taunting and criticism of you, the mark of our eternal friendship?

I who am Lillian, who am Luke, who am Asarkos, welcome you back among the living, my dear Paul, who is now Michael.

This Sarkate gave us a great deal of trouble, I'll have you know. People have become so cynical over the ages, and each time we do this it becomes harder. My Sarkate, Lillian, was herself quite a chore. Although I managed to enter her shortly after the end of her incestuous affair with her cousin, whom you now inhabit, the transfer required probing into levels of the human psyche I am loathe to ever visit again.

And yours! He was a fighter. I think his very hatred of his family kept him from despair. He so despised their example and their ways, I believe it gave him a spark we didn't anticipate. It took years to build him up just right, just so, and at the end it took extreme measures to make him surrender to the complete despair required.

I do apologize for having you wake up within a prison. But if I know you . . . and I do . . . you probably will wax nostalgic about it, and accept it happily with some philosophic twist or other. The doctor who came to you was, of course, one of ours. I had supplied him with the charism required to relieve you of your scales. He told the prison officials that you suffered from a severe case of ulcerative blepharitis, and they, not knowing anything of that ocular condition, accepted his diagnosis without much thought.

I should tell you that I greatly enjoy the sciences of this age. You will be startled by some of the technologies that have sprung up over the past two hundred years. And you will be most pleased to hear your own thoughts echoed in a theory called "evolution." Some recent thoughts about symbiotic cooperation . . . cross-species support in the development of beneficial mutations . . . have been of particular interest to me. I have incorporated them into my theories of how our two races have come to co-evolve. I will not give you the details here; I miss your company, and long to argue with you face-to-face. But I will say that not since the era when you and I turned the Cardinals and the Inquisitors against Galileo has there been so much advancement in man's sciences.

I sometimes wonder whether you think I keep returning to this world only for my own amusement. Well, perhaps, perhaps, old friend. You know me, just as I know you . . . and so I'm sure you understand that I tire of this endless, plodding migration of your people and of mine. Still, too many basic questions remain unanswered for me. So I will continue to volunteer for this mission, that I and my Asarkos companion might learn more. Even if that just means learning better questions, without learning better answers.

I am anxious to hear of the Sarkate Lillian's reunion with the spirit of the Sarkate Michael. Did you witness the meeting? I suspect there was great joy, because I know both their hearts. But I should like to hear the details from you. I long for more than my own mere supposings about what their joy in infinity is like.

In the meantime, we work to repair the very tarnished reputation we gave you. It will take me some time to explain what we needed to do, but as your release from prison indicates, progress is being made rapidly. Claims have been withdrawn, cases dropped, lies turned upside down in the past several days. It will take time, but we are young again. And we of our kind have plenty of time, don't we?

I should like to try to write another text in this lifetime. I seem unable to write anything, however, that has the universal appeal of my Gospel or my Acts of the Apostles. Those tales live forever, thanks to you.

Lazarus-Who-Is-Giselle asks me to pass along her regards. We shall visit next week, and with us will be the friend among us who is *most* anxious to see you again. Esther-Who-Is-Mousy-Girl sends her love as well.

No, that is not her real name. But I have come to call her that, and am quite fond of it.

> With you again among the Sarkate,
> Your Cousin, Friend, and Doctor, Luke

—31—

From St. Paul's first Letter To The Corinthians, Chapter 15

. . . All flesh is not the same flesh. Men have one kind of flesh, beasts have another kind, fish have another, birds another still.

Look also to the heavens: the glory of one celestial body is not the same as the glory of another.

And so it is with the resurrection of the body: flesh is created corruptible, and sown in weakness; but it is raised in power, a spiritual body.

Behold, I tell you a mystery: you shall not all fall asleep into death, but instead some shall be changed in an instant, in the twinkling of an eye, at the final trumpet.

The trumpet will sound, and the dead will be raised incorruptible, forever changed.

The corruptible flesh must accept the incorruptible. Mortality must put on immortality.

And so shall come to pass the saying, "Death is swallowed up in victory. O death, where is thy sting?"

Greet one another with a holy kiss,
Paul, an Apostle of Christ